NICK & CO. in a fix

'Oh no, not again!'
The gang groaned as the ball flew over the
gates into Mr Booth's yard. Nick and Co. were
in real trouble.

That was just the start.
When Mr Booth threatened to shut down their
youth club, the gang took action. But Nick's
Master Plan did not turn out quite as they
expected . . .

This story will appeal to anyone who has ever
said those immortal words: 'Please sir – can we
have our ball back?'

NICK & CO
in a fix

BOB CROSON

A LION PAPERBACK
Tring · Beileville · Sydney

Copyright © 1985 Bob Croson

Published by
Lion Publishing plc
Icknield Way, Tring, Herts, England
ISBN 0 85648 953 0
Albatross Books Pty Ltd
PO Box 320, Sutherland, NSW 2232, Australia
ISBN 0 86760 654 1

First edition 1985

Library of Congress Cataloging in Publication Data

Croson, Bob, 1946–
  Nick & Co. in a fix.
  (A Lion paperback)
  [1. Gang—Fiction. 2. City and town life—Fiction]
  I. Title. II. Title: Nick and Company in a fix.
  PZ7.C88237Ni 1985   [Fic]   85–13817
  ISBN 0 85648 953 0 (pbk.)

Printed and bound in Great Britain by
Cox and Wyman, Reading

CONTENTS

1 Trouble   7
2 Bad News   14
3 The Campaign Begins   23
4 The March   30
5 Nick's Master Plan   38
6 Ram's Revenge   48
7 The Piano Incident   56
8 Midnight Raid   64
9 Sparky to the Rescue   72
10 In the Dock   80
11 The Accident   87
12 Return Match   93
13 Who did it?   100
14 On the Trail   108
15 Chase   114
16 Ambush   120
17 Escape!   127
18 Nick & Co.   135

1

TROUBLE

'Give me the ball,' I screamed.

Sparky passed it to me just as he was forced against a wall by the heavy body of Franco Granelli, called 'Lump' by friend and enemy alike.

I took the ball and with clever flicks raced along the pavement carefully avoiding the potholes, lost in the dream of a Wembley Cup Final with one goal each and two minutes left: *'Nick Baker hurtles down the wing on a breakaway, the referee looks at his watch, we're almost out of time.' 'What do you think about it, Mr Clough, will he be sick as a parrot or over the moon?' 'He turns in, rounds the defender, and shoots.'*

I kicked the ball as hard as I could in the direction of Norman, our very unwilling goalkeeper. It soared high over his head and disappeared over the back of the garage gates which formed the goal.

'Now you've done it,' he said.

Adrian Blake, another of the gang, raced up. 'Hey man, why d'you do that? We'll never get it back now,' he said.

I slumped against the wall, fed up. The difference between where I thought the ball should go and where it actually went was still a bit too much for the England manager, or even Scruffy Jones, the PE master who selected the school team . . . But one day . . . All it needed was practice. I could still play for

England . . . if only I could get the stupid ball back.

'Well, who's going to face old Crabfeatures then?' asked Adrian. 'And it's not going to be me! I can still feel the clip round the ear I got last time.'

Old Crabfeatures was the owner of the garage. His more usual name was Mr Booth, and he had been very nasty to all the gang since he had bought the business a year ago.

I sat silently, with my head in my hands, desperately trying to think of a way to save face and solve the crisis. Then I had an idea. 'Let's see where it is before we do anything else. Come over here, Lump, and stand against this gate.'

Franco Granelli wandered over reluctantly. He always got roped in for this sort of thing, and he didn't like it. Just because his Dad owned the chip shop at the end of the street, 'forcing' him to 'have to' eat lots of chips, he couldn't help being a little on the large side. It was his Dad's fault.

Lump stood, facing forward and leaning with both hands against the garage gates. As nobody else volunteered to climb up I had to do it myself. Putting my hands on Lump's shoulders I leaped up. My knees dug into his back and he collapsed in a heap, with me falling heavily on top of him. He let out a great yell.

'You great wally,' I howled, rubbing my side.

'You shouldn't have put your knees in my back. How would you like it?' groaned Lump, lying like a stranded whale on the pavement.

'I suppose I had better try,' interrupted Adrian, 'before anybody else gets hurt.'

Adrian lived in Church Street, like the rest of us. He was in the same class as me and Sparky, my best

8

mate. He was very athletic and loved to run everywhere, so we all called him Whizzer. Like Norman's family, his grandparents had come over from the West Indies and settled here. Now his father had died, leaving his Mum to bring up five children, and he was the youngest. He told Lump to cup his hands and stand with his back to the gates. Then he put one foot in Lump's hands and launched himself up, grabbing for the beam above the gates. The rest of us stood back and watched in admiration. I opened my mouth to say, 'Well done, Whizzer!' when the gates opened, and there stood Mr Booth.

Lump fell backwards at Mr Booth's feet because he had been leaning against the garage gates and Whizzer was left hanging from the beam. He couldn't keep his grip, and as everybody watched him in stunned silence, his hands lost their grip. It was like slow motion in films. He fell to the ground right on top of Lump, who gasped and groaned as the wind was knocked out of him again.

'I'm sick of this. I'm not a bloomin' trampoline you know,' he complained noisily. He looked up and saw the angry face of Mr Booth looking down.

I knew what was coming next.

Sure enough, off he went!

'You lot again,' shouted Mr Booth. 'What do you think you are doing? This is private property.'

Good grief, what a bore! Always on at us.

I wanted to stand up to him, but chickened out. So I said, 'Can we have our ball back, please?'

'Now look, I'm fed up with you lot. This is the third time this week, you're nothing but a nuisance,' Mr Booth growled.

I was starting to get angry with this silly man now.

9

'But we only want our ball back,' I repeated through gritted teeth.

Mr Booth was a big brute of a man, with a bald head and a red face. He wore baggy trousers and a large brightly-coloured anorak which had seen better days. He always seemed to be angry. Well — that was the way we always saw him. Now he looked round, saw the ball lying by a pile of old tyres, and walked over to it.

'This ball you mean?' he asked. 'I'll show you what I'm going to do with this.' He picked up a sharp metal spike that was lying on the ground and fiercely pierced the ball. It burst with a loud bang. Then he threw the ball on to the heap of tyres with the spike still stuck through it.

'Now clear off,' he growled, and slammed the gates shut.

I was dumbstruck. That swine had burst our ball! I was steaming. I turned and walked quickly and angrily down the road. What else could I do? The others turned and followed me. No one said a word.

We made our way to the youth club which was by the church. It was separated from Mr Booth's garage by a plot of long grass where all the children in our street played.

When we went in, Doug Jones, the church curate, was tidying up the games cupboard helped by Sparky's sister. Her real name was Samantha, but we always called her Sam. We all liked Doug, though I did think he was a bit too religious, always going on about Jesus and God. I was also a bit miffed because Sparky spent so much time with him. Sparky went along to Doug's youth meetings at church, which were good, but I wasn't too keen to get involved like Sparky had.

But then, he's not that bad — Doug, I mean. After all, he persuaded the old lady who owned the hut and the patch of grass to let him use it for a youth club. Then he got the church and the local council to help set it up and spent a lot of his free time running it.

My pain-in-the-neck little sister, Mo, was helping too. Strictly speaking, she was too young for the club, being only seven, but she always follows me around and Doug had given up trying to keep her away.

Lots of children used the club, but me and my mates — Sparky, Whizzer, Lump, and Chip (Norman's nickname), — together with Sam and Little Mo, were the regulars. It was my gang — with me as the boss.

Anyway, we all stormed in and threw ourselves down in the old chairs. I was really mad, steaming. 'It ain't fair,' I said.

'Oh?' replied Doug from inside the cupboard.

'No, it ain't,' agreed Sparky.

Doug got up from the floor, carefully and calmly put down the table tennis bats he was holding and turned to face us. 'Would someone mind telling me what isn't fair this time?' he asked.

'Old Crabfeatures has done it again,' moaned Lump, still rubbing his bruised but ample stomach.

'Ah!' said Doug. 'Now let me see if I have the picture right.' 'You were playing football on the street outside Mr Booth's garage. Right?'

'Mm,' I grunted.

'And someone. . . ' Doug looked around at the gang's faces. I scowled. 'And someone,' he said, looking at me, 'got carried away and belted it over the fence into his yard. Right?'

11

How come he always knew? He must have second sight!

'Now he won't let you have your ball back,' continued Doug.

I was boiling inside. Why is it that adults never see the real point? 'The old faggot face did more than that,' I blurted out. 'He deliberately burst it.'

'I see,' said Doug. I don't think he did.

'Well, that wasn't fair, was it?' said Whizzer.

'No,' replied Doug. 'But he did tell you to stop playing outside his garage. You did get a warning.'

That was the end. Being patient and understanding isn't my strong point and this was too much. 'Are you on his side?' I demanded. 'It's not his road — it belongs to all of us. My Dad pays his rates as well, you know.' Then I really got going. 'Sometimes I don't understand you. You're always saying how you want to help us, you're forever reading bits of the Bible to us and trying to persuade us to go to church, but when it comes to something important, you back off.'

'Oh, come on, Nick,' Doug responded.

I was angry and upset, and couldn't think what else to do, so I decided to make a big fuss of going. 'I'm going. You don't understand,' I said. I stormed out and banged the door so hard that the wall of the hut shook. I didn't look back, but I knew the gang would follow. They'd better! And they did.

I had to do something. I didn't want my mates to see me beaten. That rat Booth was standing at the entrance to his garage. I stormed up to him. Sparky tried to stop me but I wouldn't listen.

'You toad,' I said. 'Bet your cars are all nicked old bangers.'

He turned angrily. 'What do you mean?' he

hissed. Then he stopped himself, sneered, and said, 'Go away, little boy, before I twist your scraggy little neck.'

He looked very nasty, and suddenly I felt scared. At times like this you have to resort to tried and trusted practices. I blew an enormous raspberry, and ran like fury. The rest followed at speed.

'You've not heard the last of this, you little monster,' he shouted after me.

He couldn't possibly catch me. I was beginning to feel better. But that was only the start!

2

BAD NEWS

As usual, the club was very busy. It was early evening, we had all done our homework, and were now letting off steam. Sparky and me were on the snooker table — I was winning as usual — and loads of kids were watching us and drinking cans of Coke.

Whizzer was playing non-stop table tennis with three other kids. He was so quick and never still for a moment, forcing them to go faster and faster. They were yelling and whooping with delight. Chip was by the electronic games, thumping the buttons and taking his score higher and higher. Lump just sat in a corner, watching, and eating through his usual vast quantity of crisps and chocolate before going for a bag of chips from his Dad.

Lots of kids were playing darts and dominoes, cards and other games. Some were just relaxing, listening to music. Standing by the coffee bar were Sam and Little Mo, helping Doug to sell soft drinks and crisps.

After I had done my Steve Davis on Sparky and finally potted the black, I wandered over for a refill of Coke. Sam was talking to Doug. 'You're a bit quiet tonight, Doug,' she said. 'Has the Vicar been having a go at you again? Are you in his bad books? What you done? Been riding your bike over the graves again?'

'You musn't talk about him like that. He's a very

14

kind man,' replied Doug.

'Well, he don't like us. He's always wincing when he comes in here, and wrinkles his nose like we smell or something,' said Sam.

'It's just that he finds the music a bit loud, and it's a long time since he was a kid,' said Doug, with a smile.

I couldn't picture the vicar ever being a child. As far as I was concerned he'd always been about three hundred and five years old. 'Anyway,' I butted in. 'You've still not told us why you're so grumpy.'

'I'm not grumpy. I've just had some bad news, that's all,' replied Doug solemnly.

These Christians, I thought, always pretending nothing is really wrong. Why can't they be more honest?

Doug carried on serving customers with Coke and crisps. Sam looked at me, shrugged her shoulders and tried again. 'Well, are you going to tell us then, or is it a secret?' she asked, turning to him.

'I was choosing the moment.'

'What do you mean? Is it something to do with us?' I asked, curious now.

'Yes, I'm afraid it is,' said Doug quietly. 'I had a phone call earlier today from a firm of solicitors. The old lady who owns this building has died, and it's going to be sold, together with the land between Mr Booth's garage and the church.'

'*What*?' I groaned. 'What's going to happen to us then? There's nowhere else to go.'

'I don't know,' replied Doug. 'It's a tricky one. But I do believe God will help us if we ask him.'

Some good that'll do, I thought. But as I couldn't think of anything better I kept my mouth shut and sat in a chair sulking, trying to make it look like I

15

was coming up with a master plan of my own.

As we made our way home that evening, we were all very gloomy. Hands were in pockets, heads were down. Whizzer kicked an empty can along the gutter. I felt awful.

Just as we passed the gates of Mr Booth's garage, he appeared and began to open them. He stopped, folded his arms, and looked at us. 'You must have heard the news then,' he said.

'What's it got to do with you?' I snarled.

'Oh, you'd be surprised,' smirked Mr Booth.

That man really was a toad! 'Whaddya mean?' I grunted back at him.

'Well, there's going to be an auction, isn't there?' he said.

'So what?'

'I'm going to bid for that land,' he continued. 'There aren't many people interested, so it won't fetch much. I shall buy it and tear down that rat-hole of a hut you use. Then you'll be out of my hair and I can get on with my business in peace.'

'Why, you mean thing!' said Sam, in disbelief.

'Mean, is it?' replied Mr Booth quickly. 'Well, there's nothing you can do about it!' He turned and went into his garage.

We just stood there feeling helpless. I was fuming inside, all bottled up with anger. I had to do something. I picked up Whizzer's can and hurled it through one of the garage windows. Then, realizing what I had done, rushed off, with the others close behind. Over my shoulder I could see Mr Booth coming out of his garage, shaking his fist after us.

We rounded the corner and skidded to a stop by the first lamp post. Not only was it just far enough away from Mr Booth to be safe, but I was also puffed out, and needed the support of a friendly lump of concrete.

Sparky wasn't very happy. 'Why did you do that? What good did it do? Can you see Mr Booth doing anything to help us now?' he asked, looking straight at me.

I knew underneath that Sparky was right, but I was annoyed. Annoyed with Mr Booth, with myself — and now with him. Ever since he had got too involved with Doug and become a Christian, things had not been as good between us. We had been best mates all our lives, and our Dads before us. When it came time for us to show we were the tops in the district, he was at my side. Every fight I had ever been in, there was Sparky alongside sorting somebody out.

Now he was different. I mean, I don't swear a lot, but he had stopped altogether. I even had to use Whizzer to help me with a few punch-ups because he wouldn't. There was no point in arguing with him, though, because, to cap it all, he'd even stopped shouting back at me! At first I thought it wouldn't last—I knew Sparky and I knew he couldn't keep it up, but he had! It really gets me angry now when he doesn't lose his temper.

'I suppose you're going to suggest we pray about it as well,' I said scathingly.

'Why not?' he said. 'It takes more guts than chucking cans through windows and running!'

Before I could think of a nasty answer, Sam butted in. She didn't like seeing us at each other, so she changed the subject. 'Look—we can't do anything about that at the moment, but we do have to do something about the city youth club five-a-side competition. Don't forget, Nick, you entered a team, and you also bet that stupid dope Ram that we could beat his team.'

'Mm,' I replied. This was another of those situations that my mouth had got me into. If only I could keep my big mouth shut! I don't know how Sparky manages it.

'Now, let's see,' I thought aloud. 'A team.'

'Don't forget, we need six including the sub,' said Whizzer.

'Right,' I replied. 'Now, there's me, Sparky, and you Whizzer, 'cos we're good. That's three. We need three more. Chip, you're not bad, if you concentrate.'

'Oh, it's so boring, football,' said Chip. 'Do I have to?'

'Yes,' I replied. Actually, he was not much good but there was no alternative. I could see Sam bursting to say something, and I knew what it was, so I quickly carried on speaking. 'You will be goalie, Lump. You're the right size — you fill a third of the goal just standing there,' I quipped.

Everybody laughed, except Lump. He wasn't too pleased with either the teasing or having to play, but I wasn't giving him any choice.

I still had the problem of a sixth person, and I had run out of players. I also knew what was in Sam's mind. 'We shall have to play without a sub. There isn't anybody left,' I said firmly.

Then Sam said exactly what I expected, and dreaded. 'What about me? I'm better than Lump and Chip put together,' she asked.

Now, for a girl, Sam wasn't too bad, and it was true that when she played with us, when I let her, she was better than Lump and Chip. But how could I possibly let her play in the team? I'd never hear the

18

last of it, particularly from that rat Ram. 'There's a simple answer to that — *No*. You're a girl, and girls don't play in the five-a-side competition,' I said to her.

I think I touched a nerve. Sam went berserk!

'Just because I'm a girl, what difference does it make? We have to beat Ram and his mob, it's important. You men are all the same, and it's about time you changed. I'm playing, and that's that!'

Nobody spoke. Well, what can you say?

Sam continued, 'And besides, if six don't start then you aren't allowed to carry on, it's in the rules.'

I had no answer, so against my better judgement, I gave in. 'All right,' I said. 'But I don't know how I'm gonna face Ram and his mates at school.'

'Great,' yelled Sam. 'Let's get practising.'

So we did, and I must admit — she isn't bad!

Over the next week we spent a lot of time talking and arguing about our club. For years there had been nothing in the area. My dad, who's the local policeman, had tried all sorts of things. He couldn't get anybody interested, even the council wouldn't do anything to help. Then Doug came along and set something up at the church, which was better than nothing, but still pretty hopeless. People like me feel a bit out of place in a church. After that, Doug managed to get the hut set up and we'd had our own club. Doug's good at that sort of thing. I don't understand how these things work out — he says it's through prayer and stuff like that, but I don't believe it.

Then the dreaded day came — the day of the auction. We sat with Doug on the old club chairs in the hut. Across a narrow aisle sat Mr Booth and one of his men from the garage. We called him the Hulk because of his size. There were a few people sitting behind us. At the front, by the coffee bar and behind a desk, sat a man in a smart pinstripe suit with a secretary alongside him.

The auctioneer rose to his feet. 'In accordance with the wishes of the solicitors,' he said, 'I hereby auction the property as stated in the brochure. The method of auction will be by presentation of sealed bids. I have a number of these already. Are there any more to be handed in before I close the bidding?'

'Yes,' said Doug. He got up and handed the envelope to the auctioneer's secretary.

'Any more?' he asked.

Silently Mr Booth got to his feet, looked across at Doug and the rest of us with an expression between a snarl and a sneer, and handed over an envelope to the secretary. There was a long silence as the auctioneer opened all the envelopes. After what seemed an age, he got to his feet, banged his gavel on the table, and called the meeting to order. 'As there are no more bids,' he announced, 'I hereby declare that the land and hut is sold to Mr Booth of 43 Church Street.'

There was a gasp from behind. Mr Booth got to his feet, smirked, and walked over to the auctioneer to sign the necessary papers. The gang sat in stunned silence.

Mr Booth returned down the aisle. He stopped alongside Doug, and said, very bluntly, 'I want all this lot out in one month or I will throw it out on the street.' With a nod of his head he called over the Hulk, and they walked out with an arrogant swagger.

The auctioneer picked up his things, and together

with his secretary, made his way out. As he passed us he spoke to Doug. 'Sorry about that. It was an extremely generous bid by Mr Booth, no one else came anywhere near.' He moved on and out, quietly closing the door behind him.

'What do we do now?' asked Chip.

'I don't know,' replied Doug. 'I shall have to think about it.'

I sat numb and blank, the conversations echoing in my head but seeming a long way off. It was a disaster. I had to take it out on someone, and Doug was the nearest. 'Some use the church was,' I said. 'Jesus was supposed to help those who asked,' I grumbled on.

'Did you ask him then?' replied Doug.

'That's beside the point,' I grunted back. 'You did.'

'Maybe it's not the end of the story yet,' Doug responded.

'That sounds like a cop-out to me,' I said angrily. Then I thought better. It wasn't really Doug's fault. 'I'm sorry, Doug. It's not really your fault. You've done a lot for us. We just don't want to lose the club,' I said.

There was a miserable silence, broken only by the banging of Whizzer's foot on the chair. He couldn't sit still, even now. Eventually Doug spoke. 'Come on. All is not over yet. We've still got a month left. Look, you have been a right nuisance to Mr Booth. Why don't you go and see him? Apologize for all that has happened in the past and try to persuade him to let us keep the hut. He can't be wanting it for anything, he hardly uses the buildings he's got already,' he said.

Nobody answered. They were all waiting for me.

I hated the idea but couldn't think of a better one just at that moment.

'Well, all right,' I said reluctantly. 'I don't really see why I should apologize for anything. I've done nothing wrong, much. But if it means keeping the club, I'll do it.'

'Right,' said Doug. 'I'll ring him and make an appointment.'

3

THE CAMPAIGN BEGINS

We stood around in the club hut feeling uncomfortable and edgy. Sparky was aimlessly bouncing a ball against the cushion of the pool table; Whizzer was batting a table tennis ball up in the air over and over again. Lump was stuffing himself with chocolate.

Then the door opened and Doug walked in. He had his crash helmet under his arm. 'Sorry I'm late,' he said, as he put his helmet down on the coffee-bar. 'Right. Let's get going.'

'I'm not at all sure about this,' I muttered. The more I thought about it, the more stupid the idea seemed.

'Do you want a club or not?' asked Doug. 'Because if you do, you should be willing to swallow your pride and try anything.'

He had a point. I owed it to everybody to try. 'Oh all right, let's get it over with,' I said, with a sigh.

It had been agreed that me and Sparky, together with Sam, would go along with Doug to see Mr Booth. Reluctantly, we followed Doug along the road to the garage. We passed the main gates and made our way to the small office alongside the open stretch of concrete where second-hand cars stood ready for sale. I felt funny inside, scared and angry all mixed up together.

Doug knocked politely on the glass door. I could see Mr Booth sitting behind his desk, but he had his back to us and was looking into a filing cabinet. He turned in his chair in response to the knock, a smile on his face. He must have been expecting a customer. The smile quickly changed to a scowl when he saw Doug, me, Sparky and Sam. 'Oh, it's you. You'd better come in,' he said.

Boy, what a toad, I thought.

We went in, Doug leading the way.

'Well, you asked to see me, and time is money, so get on with it,' said Mr Booth gruffly, leaning back in his chair.

There was a long silence.

Mr Booth looked at us. Sam and Sparky looked at the floor. I pursed my lips and stared hard at the wall behind his head thinking, 'What on earth am I doing here?' and, 'Here's another fine mess you got me into,' and other equally useless and irrelevant thoughts. Doug was looking at each of us in turn, desperately willing one of us to say something.

The silence was getting embarrassing. I knew it was up to me really, so I sucked in a big breath of air and began. 'We have come to apologize for any trouble we may have caused you and your garage, and promise we won't do it again,' I said quickly and breathlessly.

'Huh, I should think so, and about time too,' answered Mr Booth.

'And,' I went on, 'And to ask you if you would let us keep the hut in the corner of the land by the church. We promise that we won't interfere with anything to do with the garage, play outside, or cause any sort of bother.' I sucked in a great breath of air, relieved to have finished.

'I see,' replied Mr Booth slowly. 'If I allow you to keep the hut, you won't cause any bother.'

'Yes, that's right,' butted in Sam hopefully.

Mr Booth got to his feet, put both hands on his desk, and glowered at us. 'I don't respond to blackmail,' he barked. 'What you're saying is that if I don't let you keep the hut, you will cause a lot of trouble around the garage!'

'No, no, we . . .' began Sparky.

'Let me tell you,' continued Mr Booth, 'that if there is the slightest bit of trouble anywhere *near* the garage, I will use any method I like to stop it, and I don't need your protection. It strikes me that some of you lot need a rattling good hiding.' He looked straight at me, then he turned his anger on Doug. 'And as for you, Vicar, or curate, or whatever you call yourself, I didn't think blackmail was part of the church's business.'

'I think you're missing the point,' put in Doug.

'On the contrary, I think I'm only too well aware of the point,' replied Mr Booth quickly. 'There is no way that hut will remain. You have three weeks and two days to remove all of your equipment. I want no more bother from you or any of these young ruffians.' He waved his arm in our direction.

'I think you're being rather unfair,' said Doug.

'That's enough,' grunted Mr Booth. 'I have bought the property, you get out. Now go away, I have got work to do and you are stopping me from doing it.' He thumped the table.

Sam turned abruptly and rushed out crying. Sparky followed her silently. Doug pushed me out, but he wasn't quick enough. I had something to say to Booth, and nothing was going to stop me. I was going to give him something in return for what he had got to say. 'You're a rotten, mean, nasty swine,' I said, desperately struggling for words. 'And I'll get my own back on you for this.'

Doug forced me through the doorway, and shut the door. Mr Booth stood at his desk, hands on hips, and looked through the glass door with a surly smirk.

Doug managed to drag me away. I felt like kicking and screaming.

Back in the hut, the rest were waiting.

'What happened?' asked Whizzer.

We just slumped in the chairs and didn't say a word. Nobody moved for a long while, apart from the odd swinging foot or tapping finger. I was boiling up inside. In my head many thoughts were bubbling and brewing, all nasty. Why are adults so unreasonable? Old Booth could have let us stay. I bet there's something fishy going on in his garage that he doesn't want anybody to know about. We didn't do anything to him — well, not much. I'll get my own back on him. I'll make him wish he'd never done and said those things. What we need is to get organized for some action, our way! It's time for me to take a grip on the situation.

'I'm not finished yet,' I said, the thoughts whirling through my mind. 'I'm not going down without a fight. Look, if you're with me then meet me on the street tonight at six o'clock.'

I turned towards Doug. 'I'm sorry Doug,' I said. 'It's not your fault, but we're going to do it my way. When someone gets nasty, you have to get nasty back, or they walk all over you.' I got up and walked to the door. 'Anyone coming?' I asked, but was really telling.

'What about helping Doug with all the moving that has to be done?' asked Sam. I wasn't in the mood for co-operation.

Sparky turned to me. I could see that he was upset. 'I'm not going to leave Doug in the lurch,' he said, 'just because you've lost your temper. This is no way to treat a friend who's done a lot for you.'

I was confused, mad, and upset, and didn't know how to answer that one. There was a sort of empty pause.

Then Doug said, 'I have persuaded the church to let us start a more limited club in the church hall and meeting rooms. We have to agree to stop some of the more noisy activities, and we can only meet two nights each week, and we have to clear everything away afterwards, but it's better than nothing.'

He shouldn't have said that. I had been beginning to wilt, but that finished me off. I remembered all the trouble we had before. I turned to the others. 'You can do what you like,' I said. 'But I'm off. I'll see you tonight if you really want to do something to sort this out.' I didn't know what I was going to do, but I'd think of something.

That evening at six o'clock I met the others on the street and began to plan a campaign. I knew Sparky wasn't keen, but at least he came.

'I've been thinking,' I began. 'What we need is some publicity. I've seen it on telly. First we organize a petition, get as many names as we can, then we take the names in a march to the City Hall.'

'Sounds a bit far-fetched to me,' grumbled Lump.

'Oh shut up, Lump,' put in Sam. 'If anyone mentions work you have a heart failure. I think it's a great idea.'

'What's your dad going to say?' retorted Lump. He really is a wet blanket on anything, except for food that is.

'I know what my dad will say,' added Chip. 'He'll go crackers.'

'Well, I think it's great, man,' said Whizzer. 'Lots of fun and a good rumble.' He turned to Chip. 'Your dad's just scared because he thinks he might lose his job if he gets involved in anything risky,' he said.

Lump asked me again, 'But what will your dad say?'

I didn't really want to think about that one, but the best form of defence is attack, so I attacked Lump.

I put my face a short distance from his. 'I'm not going to be put off,' I said. 'I'm not going to let Booth or anybody walk all over us. He plays mean, so will I. Anyway, what can go wrong? Dad's always telling me about democracy and freedom in this country — that's why he's a copper. Well, I just want a piece of it for us. He can't argue with that.'

'I just don't think he'll see it that way,' replied Lump.

What a softie! What did it matter what my dad thought? 'I'm fed up with this,' I said. 'Are we doing it or not?'

In their own way they all eventually agreed, although some were not too happy about it, and Sparky insisted on telling Doug.

We set about organizing the petition first, taking sheets of paper and getting lots more local kids as well to help. Then we canvassed the whole area, getting people to sign. We stood outside the local shops and knocked on lots of doors.

My dad didn't really mind this. He had heard all about Mr Booth, and wasn't too keen on the man himself. We weren't doing any harm, and he had a word with the other local policemen to keep an eye on us. It was a good job he didn't know about the march, though. That would have been a different story. Before long, we had everything ready. It was too late to go back now. Anyway, nothing could possibly go wrong. Could it?

4

$\diamond$

THE MARCH

Getting the petition together had been hard work. But we had enjoyed it. Now we had two huge boxes full of assorted bits of paper with the signatures of all the local people who could be persuaded to sign. In an empty shed at the bottom of Whizzer's extremely overgrown garden, we had made placards and banners out of old sheets and canes, taken with some stealth from under the noses of curious mums.

It was the final meeting before the march. I got there first and unlocked the door. I could hear Lump coming from a long way off with a crackle of crisp paper and thud of heavy feet crashing through the assorted rubbish at the bottom of the garden. I opened the door just as Lump arrived.

'Can't you be quieter?' I demanded.

'I was being,' replied Lump innocently.

There was no point in going on about it, that was Lump! Quietly, Sparky and Sam slipped in behind Lump through the door. 'Come on, you two, we haven't got time to waste,' said Sam as she and Sparky unfurled the banner they were working on. It was fortunate for her that I was busy or that remark would have earned her a thick ear, girl or no girl!

It was not long before Chip arrived, and Little Mo as well. He set to work on a placard, while Little Mo wandered around getting in everybody's way. Sisters!

Eventually Whizzer arrived, wearing a pair of headphones, and clicking his fingers to the Reggae music which only he could hear. One thing Whizzer could never do was arrive on time, and he got a mouthful from me every time he let us down, but it made no difference.

'Where have you been?' I demanded.

Whizzer swayed with the music and smiled.

I reached over and switched the small cassette off.

'Hi, man,' he beamed.

'You're late,' I grunted. 'This isn't a game you know.'

'OK, man, OK, keep cool, don't panic,' replied Whizzer. 'Whaddya want me to do?'

'Shut up and listen for a start,' was my curt reply. Nobody was taking it as seriously as me. Didn't they realize how important this was? But the gang sensed the edge in my voice and everyone stopped and listened to my instructions for the march.

'Right. In the morning I want everybody outside the doors of the club by ten o'clock. Whizzer, Lump, Chip, you bring along the banners. Sparky, you and Sam bring the boxes of signatures. Remember, we only want club regulars along on the march. Get as many as you can, but only club members! Nothing can go wrong if we do it properly. My dad says everybody has a right to demonstrate peacefully, and the trouble with marches is that they are badly organized. Well, we won't be. So, he'll be happy then.'

'Are you going to tell your dad?' asked Chip.

Trust him to ask that! 'I might,' I replied. 'He's told me lots of times about people's freedoms and rights. Well, I'm taking him at his word.'

'My dad's going to be hopping mad,' said Chip ruefully.

'You're not backing out, are you?' I asked sharply.

'No,' replied Chip weakly. 'Just anticipating a sore backside!'

He's not the only one, I thought to myself. Then I said out loud, 'Let's get everything finished and go home. And remember, don't tell *anyone*, except club members!'

They all finished off their tasks and left, except for Sam, Sparky, and me. We tidied up then left, locking the door and leaving through the broken back fence of Whizzer's house.

Something was troubling Sparky, I could feel it. We walked along as far as the gates of our houses not saying anything. Sam knew something was wrong and walked off quickly, saying, 'See you tomorrow.'

I stood with Sparky. He needed to say something. I didn't know what, but I figured I had better let him get it over with. I didn't have long to wait!

'You're doing this all wrong,' he said.

'You got a better way?' I asked. Before he had a chance to start I said, 'And don't go on about turning the other cheek and all that stuff. I'm not a Christian, and I don't want to be. Every time I turn the other cheek someone slaps that one as well!'

I was defensive because inside I was beginning to have my doubts about the whole thing. But I couldn't back down now — a man's got his pride! Everybody would think I was chicken, and I wouldn't be able to lift my head on the street.

'Look, we're only going to upset more and more

people doing it this way,' said Sparky, 'and I bet Ram gets involved and causes trouble, too'.

'That's a risk we'll have to take. I'm not backing down now,' I replied. 'And don't you dare say anything to anybody or I'll never speak to you again.'

Sparky stood silently. 'All right,' he said eventually. 'So long as you don't do anything daft.' He turned and walked in.

Boy, friends are really funny sometimes. They always want it their own way!

The next morning was grey, damp, and very unwelcoming. Usually on a Saturday my mum has a terrible time trying to get me out of bed, but I was up and dressed and ready to go before she had even focused.

She knew I was up to something, but none of the usual tactics worked to find out what was going on. Little Mo was the usual informer, but not today. All she said to Mum was, 'You'll have to wait and see.'

We left the house to head for the club. In my mind I had the picture of a great march to the City Hall, meeting the Mayor, handing over the petition, being promised the club would be saved at all cost, and returning shoulder-high in triumph.

I turned the corner of the road in this glowing anticipation, and was pulled back to reality by Little Mo tugging at my sleeve. I looked ahead and gasped. Ahead of me the road was full of kids. There must have been at least two hundred. Brightly-coloured banners broke through the grey of the day as people jostled about, laughing and talking, making too much noise. I pushed my way through to the steps of the club where the rest of the gang were.

'What happened?' I demanded. 'I said only club members.'

'I guess there were more club members than we thought,' replied Chip helplessly.

'Hey, man, what does it matter?' said Whizzer. 'We'll sure make an impact with this lot.'

I felt uneasy about the whole thing, but there was no way back now. Things had gone too far. Sparky looked sick.

I shouted out, 'Quiet!' and then louder, 'QUIET!'

'Now, everyone get in fours, no more than four in a row, follow the people in front, and don't do anything daft,' I shouted.

Slowly, everyone milled round until there was some sort of order. Then I gave the order to move off.

All went well as we passed through our district. When we reached the park on the edge of the main shopping area of the city I decided to walk back along the column to see how things were. I was horrified. As we had marched, other local kids had joined in, so there was now a huge crowd. Worse still, in the middle of the column, was my hated enemy Ram, together with some of his mates. I knew they were out to cause trouble. He smirked at me.

'Don't cause any trouble, Ram. This isn't the place to sort out our differences, it's too important,' I said firmly.

'What, me?' replied Ram sarcastically. 'I've only come to help.'

His mates jeered and chanted. I realized there was nothing I could do, and went back to the front of the march. I told Sparky and the others what was happening further back. Little Mo suggested that we might try what Doug would do in such a situation — pray — but I shut her up with a gruff, 'Don't be stupid.' Inside however, I was thinking of a quick prayer, just in case.

As we reached the shopping area the chanting grew louder. The orderly procession of four in a row broke up as Ram and his mates jostled the marchers. They started shouting and swearing. It wasn't long before a police car turned up to investigate, followed by more cars as the word was spread by police radio.

Where the road narrowed near the front of the big department stores, a posse of police were waiting. It was a big relief to me that my dad wasn't one of them. They stopped us and wanted to know what we were doing, so I told them. The sergeant in charge wasn't very pleased that they hadn't been given advance warning, but accepted my explanation.

'I want twenty only to carry on to the City Hall,' he said. 'And the rest to go back to the park and wait.'

This seemed a good idea to me, so I passed on the message. Ram had other ideas. Suddenly, from among the mass of kids, a brick was hurled through the nearest shop window. It broke with an awful crash. As if they were at a football match, Ram and his pals used the tactic of surging the children round like a stampede of cattle, all in different directions. More windows were smashed and people were knocked to the ground. The noise, shouting, and screaming was terrible.

I just looked on in absolute horror. I mean, I'm no angel, but I had never been involved in anything like this before. Before long, lots more police arrived and we were all herded back to the park.

All of the gang, including Sam and Little Mo, ended up at the police station. We were asked lots of questions and then told to sit and wait on a long wooden bench in the entrance. I was terrified that Dad would walk in any moment and I wasn't looking forward to it. I was also very angry and frustrated. Even some of the kids themselves didn't care about losing the club. Why were so many people uncaring and selfish?

A door opened, and my father appeared. He didn't look too pleased. 'In here, you lot,' he ordered. We shuffled past him into the room and turned to face him.

'What on earth do you think you are doing?' he demanded. 'Don't tell me,' he turned to me, 'I don't need to guess very hard to find out who's behind it.' My dad always looks large and frightening in his policeman's uniform. I could tell that some of the others were scared stiff and near to tears. But not me!

'We did what was right,' I blurted out. 'We didn't do anything wrong. We can't help it if trouble-makers do things like that. Somebody's got to care and somebody's got to do something.'

'Shut up Nick. I'll talk to you later,' cut in Dad. I was angry but did as I was told. 'I'm not wasting time on you all now,' he added. 'Fortunately, the sergeant spoke up for you and said that you had nothing to do with the broken windows and other damage. You will all go straight home now and I shall see each of your parents to tell them what has happened and let them deal with you all.' He paused. 'Now go home,' he said.

We all turned and shuffled out slowly. I didn't dare think about what he'd do to me later. I knew it wouldn't be pleasant!

5

◇

NICK'S MASTER PLAN

We walked home very slowly. It's funny how distances seem greater when you're feeling depressed, and it was an awful long time before we came to our street. I was miserable and walked along the gutter kicking a stone. Nobody spoke. We were all thinking about what our parents would say.

Suddenly from behind me there was a fierce 'PARP!!' A huge low-loader lorry passed by and I jumped on to the pavement for safety. 'Idiot,' I yelled, and shook my fist. It was carrying a very big, yellow earthmover, and I wondered what on earth that was doing down our road.

It wasn't long before I found out. It drew to a halt alongside the land between the club and Mr Booth's garage, behind some other vans and cars. A group of men stood around talking and the driver joined them.

'What's going on?' I said to the others. Immediately we all broke into a run in the direction of the activity and noise. As we got nearer we could see what was happening. The grassy area was already churned up and machines were scraping the ground flat.

I butted into the group of men talking by the parked vehicles. 'What are you doing?' I demanded.

A large, red-faced man turned his head. 'Shove off, kid,' he said.

'Look, mate,' I replied, 'there's no need to be like that, tell us what's going on.'

The man turned right round now and looked at us all aggressively. 'Mr Booth warned us there might be some trouble from local kids, and you fit the description of the ringleaders. Now get lost!'

He turned away and then turned back again. 'You might as well know that we have orders to pull down that hut over there tomorrow,' he grunted, jerking his thumb. Then he turned again to carry on his chat with the others.

We stood, stunned that the crunch had finally come and the club was finished. I couldn't bear to watch, and turned away in the direction of home. First, the disaster of the march — and now this!

Running through my head were thoughts of home and what was going to happen, the disasters of the day, and images of the club building being ripped down. I could have cried, but I knew I couldn't. Everyone would think I was a softy. To stop myself from blubbering I tried to think of ways to get back at Mr Booth. I knew it was hopeless but I couldn't bear the thought of that horrible man winning.

Then it came to me — a last defiant act of heroism in the face of defeat. Custer's last stand. It was my Master Plan. We would have to sit-in! I turned to the others and told them my idea.

'Let's organize a sit-in!' I said, trying to make it sound really exciting.

The groans were loud and long. 'You must be joking,' replied Chip.

'What a load of softies,' I cut in, stung by their defeated attitude. 'Come on, we're not going to give in without a fight, are we?'

'Yes,' said Lump bluntly.

'Give me one good reason why we shouldn't?' I demanded, ignoring Lump.

'I'll give you two,' put in Sparky. 'One, it's stupid, and two, it's wrong.'

'Well, I think we should,' added Sam, loyally. 'Why should we let him win that easily?'

At last, someone on my side. If this goes on much longer, I thought, I shall have to revise my opinion of girls. But I mustn't allow a crisis to colour my judgements too much!

I could see the others squirming a bit in embarrassment. 'Well, look at that,' I said. 'The only one with any guts is Sam. I know what you lot are afraid of — you're scared of getting a good hiding. Well, you're going to get one anyway, so why the fuss? It'll be tomorrow before my dad tells your parents, and by that time we'll have started the sit-in. They won't punish you twice, so what are you afraid of?' I could see the heads beginning to nod. 'I'm the only one who's going to be punished tonight,' I continued, 'and I'm not scared.' I was, I was terrified, but I wouldn't let on.

There was a silence, ended by Sparky. 'But it's still wrong! It's stupid really,' he added. 'We can't win and it'll only mean more trouble.'

I was really mad with Sparky. For a best pal he was being very difficult. He might have been right, but that wasn't the point, was it? I hated myself for saying it, but I just lost my temper. 'If you're not with me, you can get lost!' I said.

He turned, then looked back to say something, but stopped himself, and walked off slowly down the street.

'You tell anybody and I'll thump you,' I shouted after him. To the others I said, 'I want to see you all at midnight round the back of the club hut, and not a word.'

Everyone nodded, some more willingly than others, then turned for their homes. Sam walked alongside me. 'We'll show 'em, you and me, won't we, Nick?' she said.

'Mm,' I replied. I hoped she wasn't getting the wrong idea. Thank goodness Little Mo was there to protect me!

When Little Mo and I got home the inevitable happened. Mo was sent straight to bed with a smacked bottom and no supper. I was sent to my room to wait for Dad to come home. It wasn't long before I heard the bang of the front door, and after hearing heated discussions downstairs, the call came for me.

'Nick, down here, now!' They must have heard Dad's voice three streets away! I came downstairs, trying to look as apologetic as I possibly could. Experience told me not to argue but to keep my mouth shut and take the punishment.

Dad blasted me out. I don't know what he said because I sort of switch off and just watch the mouth movements in a kind of hypnotic stare. Then the inevitable happens. The wooden spoon is ritually taken from the kitchen drawer and I am forced to bend over with his heavy hand on my neck. It's funny, you don't really feel it after the first one, but it's best to make some sort of noise or he claims it as a miss and adds one on at the end.

I always cry. It's expected. Anyway, it hurts as the numbness wears off. Then I'm sent to bed with the usual line of 'it hurts me more than it hurts you'. Who believes that? What gets me is that Grandma reckons no one was as bad as my dad when he was a child, but he never mentions that. As far as he is concerned, nobody has ever been as bad as me. It doesn't seem right somehow!

At midnight I was woken by my alarm clock. I had wrapped it in a scarf. Now for my Master Plan — the sit-in. I had insisted to Little Mo that she shouldn't come because the route out of the house was dangerous. Carefully I climbed out of my bedroom window, over the kitchen roof, along the top of the garden wall, and dropped to the ground in the back alley. Then I quietly plodded down the street, hopped over the fence and round to the back of the club hut.

Sam and Whizzer were already there. Chip followed me in, and eventually Lump arrived, muttering about the cold, and how stupid all this was, and why on earth he had let himself be talked into this, until I shut him up with a threat.

I broke the lock on the back door with a brick, and we eased it open. We had brought a couple of torches, and using them for light, I gave everybody orders and we set to work. The few old bits of furniture left were heaped against the two doors. Fortunately the side windows were boarded up anyway because they kept getting broken. Then I called everybody together again.

'Chip, you take the first watch while we all get some sleep. After half an hour wake up Whizzer to take over, then Sam, Lump, and me,' I said. 'We'll keep that up till the first workmen arrive. When they do, we stand behind the two front windows and chant. Try and think of something good to chant.'

Sam, Whizzer, Lump and I sat against the wall of the hut and tried to sleep, but it was impossible, so after a while we all kept watch together. The street outside was eerie and empty, very much quieter than usual, with pools of orange light around each lamp stand. We were all cold, tired and miserable. Somehow, I wished Sparky was with us. He always cheered me up. Maybe he had been right. It didn't seem such a good idea now, but I tried to keep everybody going with occasional comments about Mr Booth, and stories of some of the great things that had happened at the club. I was convinced Mr Booth was up to no good, and the more I thought about him in those boring hours, the more I became sure he was some sort of criminal. But what sort? And how could I prove it?

After what seemed ages, the dawn began to break and the lamps switched themselves off. Lump and Chip wanted to give up but I bullied them to continue. As for Whizzer — well, he always treats everything as a lot of fun, however serious it is. Only Sam was taking the thing really seriously. People were beginning to appear on the street — the early risers off to work, the milkman, and the newspaper delivery boy. I wondered what would happen at home when they found out I'd disappeared. Boy, would I get in trouble this time! My bottom was still sore from the last onslaught, so I guessed a few more smacks with the wooden spoon wouldn't make much difference. I could feel the others getting tense and anxious.

'Let's warm up with a good song,' I said, hoping to raise their spirits. I broke into, 'We shall not, we shall not be moved,' and the others followed, rather half-heartedly.

Suddenly a van drew up and we stopped abruptly. As we watched in silence, the men got out and stretched. The big fellow who had spoken to us the day before got out. He must have been the foreman — I could hear him barking out orders. Then he walked over towards the door of the hut and we instinctively ducked down. He turned the key in the lock, twisted the handle, and pushed. 'That's funny,' he said, 'it was all right yesterday.'

He then tried his shoulder against the door. I could see the furniture we had piled up beginning to move, so I decided it was time for action. I jumped up and shouted, 'You can't come in!'

The man leapt back in amazement. 'Who's that?' he shouted.

Stupidly, I replied, 'It's me!'

'Who's me?' he went on.

This was getting silly.

'We are the members of this club and you can't pull it down. This is a sit-in,' I shouted.

There was a pause.

'Come on out!' the man barked. 'Don't be stupid.' Then he started to get angry. 'If you don't come out this moment, I shall call the police.'

'Go away,' I replied. Then we all began to sing:

'We shall not, we shall not be moved,
We shall not, we shall not be moved,
This is our club and we'll not let you knock
*   it down.*
We shall not be moved.'

The man walked away back to the rest of the workmen. He was pointing and talking, but we couldn't hear what he was saying. One man went off down the road. Soon Mr Booth appeared. He came up to the window and glared in.

'Oh, not you again,' he groaned, looking me

44

straight in the eye. 'Now, you just get out of there. I've had enough of all this. I've a good mind to come in and sort you out myself.' He looked very fierce and angry and I knew he meant it.

'You touch me and I'll have the law on you. My dad's a policeman you know,' I replied quickly.

This seemed to calm him down a bit and he stepped back to talk to the others. Then he returned. 'I want you out in five minutes, or I call the police,' he demanded.

Our only reply was another chorus of 'We shall not, we shall not be moved'.

Mr Booth stood back with the rest of the men looking angrily in our direction. I wondered what he was going to do. Then I saw Little Mo and Dad rushing down the street. Dad was half-dressed and obviously angry. I could see him talking to Mr Booth, then he marched up to the door and thumped on it.

'Nick, Nick! Come out here this minute,' he shouted. For my own safety I decided this wasn't a wise move, and anyway, it would be giving in.

'No, Dad!' I shouted back, 'I'm not. We are fighting for our rights here, and we're not coming out.'

He thumped even harder. 'You get out here this minute,' he shouted, 'or I'll write your principles on your backside with a wooden spoon.'

'You're going to do that anyway,' I replied, 'and besides, what about all those principles and rights you're always telling me about?'

He thumped the door again, and then backed away to the pavement.

I hadn't noticed before, but all the other parents had arrived, together with Doug and Sparky. They seemed to be having some kind of argument, but I couldn't hear them. Doug was talking. People were waving their arms about and the voices were very loud. I could see Doug was trying to calm them all down. Eventually he came towards the window and looked in. 'Nick, you there?' he called.

'Yes,' I replied, aggressively.

'OK,' he said. 'Listen, you've made your protest, and I really appreciate it, but things are getting serious.'

'Good!' I grunted.

'Look, Nick,' Doug went on, 'if you carry on, you'll ruin any chance of setting up a smaller club in the church and you'll also do your own cause no good. Don't expect publicity, or sympathy, you won't get it. If you leave now, then your parents have promised not to punish you, and Mr Booth has said he won't take things any further. But if it goes on, the police will have to be called and your parents will punish you as well.'

'Blackmail,' I retorted.

'Think it over,' he said. 'I'll be back in five minutes.'

I turned to the others. One look told me it was a lost cause. I could see they wanted to give up — all except Sam, loyal as ever.

'I think we should take Doug's advice,' said Chip.

'Me too,' added Lump quickly.

Whizzer didn't really mind, but didn't want to upset his mum any more.

I paused. 'OK,' I said eventually, and we pulled the barricade down and opened the door.

We went out silently and joined our parents who took us off home. I looked hard at Sparky, who just looked sad. I couldn't bear to watch as I heard the bulldozer start up and the sound of splintering wood and cracking glass. I fought back tears of bitterness.

It was a sad day for Nick and Co. What was even worse, was that Dad broke his promise. He didn't hit me; he did something far worse. He had promised me a dog on my next birthday but now he said that I couldn't have one if I got into any more bother. That really got to me! No way could I avoid trouble — that's impossible!

6

RAM'S REVENGE

I didn't go along to the new club set up in the church
hall for a while. But then I decided I'd better go
along. I was getting very bored at home, and the
others seemed to be having a good time at the club.
Anyway, I didn't want to lose my position as leader
of the gang.

We could only meet twice a week in the church
hall and everything had to be put away each time. It
all seemed a bit wet to me and pretty useless. Things
usually turn out that way when grown-ups get their
hands on them, I thought.

The church hall was a big room with a high
ceiling, and was painted in bright colours. It had a
stage at one end which was used by the drama club
and for the big meetings the church had every week.
That first time back I paced around and made my
presence felt, just to let everybody know I was there.
The tuck shop had been set up in the kitchen so I
went in to buy a drink.

'Hello Nick,' said a voice from the corner of the
room. I turned round and saw Aunty Edna. She
wasn't my real Aunty, nor the Aunty of any of the
other kids, but we all called her that. She was great.
Sometimes we visited her in her little old house at the
bottom of the street, and she always had some pop
or sweets for us. I had no idea how old she was, but
she must have been ancient because she was my

48

father's Aunty Edna before me.

'Hello,' I replied, rather grumpily.

'What's the matter with you, as if I didn't know,' she continued. 'You're just like your father before you — pig-headed and stubborn.' If it had been anybody else, I would have been very rude, but not to Aunty Edna! 'When will you learn?' she went on. 'Everybody's on your side, really. You just have to realize you may not know best all the time.'

I let her go on, but I didn't really listen. Old people do go on a bit, either about how much better, or worse, things were when they were young; or they talk at great length about their illnesses. They think they know it all.

'I don't know,' she said, shaking her head.

Just then Sam popped her head round the door and rescued me. 'Hey, have you forgotten the five-a-side competition?' she asked.

'Oh, right,' I replied, in relief. Before she had a chance to say anything, I said to Aunty Edna, 'See you! Got to get a team organized.' I moved out of the room as quickly as I could and didn't look back.

As the team-sheet had already been handed in I couldn't knock Sparky's name off, and anyway we would have really been in a mess without him because he was a good footballer. But I still wasn't feeling that friendly towards him. I just can't understand people being so unwilling to change, and so stubborn.

I got everybody together and told them what we were going to do, then we went out to the park to practise. Lump was hopeless as usual, but at least his vast bulk blocked quite a bit of the goal. The only problem was, he tended to jump out of the way if the ball was kicked too hard. Chip made an effort for once and wasn't too bad. Whizzer and Sparky were both very good, as usual.

Sam? Well, she was skilful and sharp, but I wasn't going to tell her that! When she asked how well she had played I told her that although she had tried hard, it wasn't quite good enough and she would be the reserve. I could see that this made her really mad. She knew that I would do almost anything to avoid her actually playing, so I quickly got involved in the football to avoid confrontation.

The day of the competition was hot and sultry. The team met outside the church. Doug had persuaded our school to lend us some kit for the occasion. It was all red. I felt great when I tried it on in front of the mirror at home, pretending I was playing for Liverpool.

On the way to the park we all talked excitedly about the competition ahead and our chances. I was sure we could win this year if everybody tried hard. The park was very busy. It had been taken over for the competition and several pitches had been marked out. In the middle was a large white tent where the organizers worked it all out.

We were organized into four leagues, the winning teams making up the semi-final placings. Fortunately, we were not drawn against Ram's team. Nobody really liked playing against them because they were dirty and mean. As we waited and talked we didn't notice Ram and his mates making their way across the park to the organizer's marquee. The first we knew was a yelp of pain from Chip as Ram kicked him from behind.

'Oh, so sorry! Didn't notice you there,' he said, with an evil smirk on his face.

There are some kids you just can never get on with, and this creep was the king. 'Why don't you shove off?' I said.

'What's the matter, sonny?' he replied sarcastically. 'Still crying over losing your little doll's house — sorry — club hut?'

That did it. I was really angry now as I remembered what he had done to us on the march. 'You pig,' I said. 'I won't forget the trouble you caused on our march. I'll get you for that. Now, push off, before I put my foot in your face.'

Ram was always tougher with his cronies round him, and today was no exception. 'You better button your lip, worm,' he grunted, 'or I might have to do it for you. You know what your trouble is,' he added, 'you just can't take a joke.' He turned to his pals and smirked. They laughed obediently, the stupid dopes.

I wasn't going to back down, never, and stood up against him. 'You just clear off,' I said. 'I'm not afraid of you.'

'You should be,' he said, with a sneer.

I could sense a fight brewing. I didn't think we'd win with Sparky the way he was, but I would never back down. Just at that moment there was an announcement over the tannoy: 'Would all teams who have not yet reported to the administration tent, please do so immediately?' demanded a voice.

Ram looked me up and down, then said, 'I'll see to you later. Come on, men.' He turned to go.

Why couldn't I learn to keep my mouth shut? Like a fool I had to take it further. 'I'll be waiting,' I said arrogantly.

'You do that,' he replied. Then, as a parting shot, he moved forward and kicked Chip's leg again. 'Oh, so sorry, it was an accident,' he said. 'I'm so clumsy.'

Chip rolled in agony as they strolled away, laughing to each other. I would have gone after Ram but the others stopped me. I didn't have time to think up any plans for revenge. We were due to play the first round then. We played very well through all the qualifying rounds, with Sparky and Whizzer whipping down the wings, and me in the middle spraying the ball about and cutting back to help in defence where Chip was doing a sterling job in spite of his injury. Lump worked hard in goal and made some quite good saves — sometimes with very unusual parts of his anatomy.

We won our group and reached the semi-final. We were playing against a club from the other side of the city. In spite of having the first goal scored against us, we managed to pull one back so that, with five minutes to go, it was one goal each.

Chip was limping so badly I didn't think he would make it to the end of the game. With two minutes to go they nearly scored but Lump's ample bulk got in the way and the ball rebounded to Chip. He took off like I've never seen him do before, completely fogetting his limp and, after passing several players, made a superb shot that whistled into a corner of the goal. When we had got over our astonishment we leaped for joy and smothered Chip. There wasn't even enough time to restart. When he eventually surfaced we could see that Chip wasn't too well. That last great effort had finished him off and he was in real agony from the damaged leg.

A St John's ambulance man came over to have a look and said Chip couldn't play in any more matches and strapped his leg up with heavy bandages. To make matters worse, the team that won in the other semi-final was none other than Ram's lot. Just our luck! I could have coped with Sam playing in some earlier round. I could just about handle having her in the team for the final, in an emergency. But against Ram's team no way! They would make mincemeat of her. But Sam had other ideas. This was her big chance, and she wasn't going to let it slip. What could I do? I seriously thought of scratching from the competition, but neither Sam, nor my pride, would allow it.

It was time for the final. We marched on to the pitch and took up positions. I could hear murmurs from the crowd as they noticed that one of the team was a girl. It made me squirm with embarrassment. Then Ram's team sauntered out. We looked smart in our bright red gear; they looked like an advert for a rag market, just about managing the same colour — a sort of faded, dirty blue.

Ram looked across at us and sneered. The whistle blew and he and I made our way to the middle to meet the referee.

'This isn't right,' he complained. 'He's got a girl in his team. 'It's not a Brownies' tea-party, you know.'

I was somewhere between embarrassment and anger, and didn't quite know what to say. I heaved a sigh of relief when the referee rescued me. 'There's nothing against it in the rules, so I suggest we get on with the game,' he said straightforwardly.

' 'Ere, hang about,' said Ram. 'I hope that there's going to be no favouritism then, when we tackle her and all that.'

'There won't be,' replied the ref. 'Now, let's get on with it.'

Poor Sam, I thought, I shall have to try and protect her. But then there was no time to think about it, the toss had been made and we were quickly under way.

Ram's lot were really rough, and they set about us straight away. I wasn't sure what was kicked the most — the ball, or our shins. I could feel myself getting angry. The referee didn't seem to be doing much about the pushing or kicking. Then he started telling me off for arguing. Why didn't he tell them off for kicking? Yet another stupid grown-up that couldn't grasp the first principles of fairness! I mean, the only kicking that I did was in retaliation.

Up to half-time there was no score, but we'd lost a lot of blood. In the second half they continued in the same way. They were really pushing Sam around and I thought once or twice she might cry, but she didn't. Then came my moment of glory. Lump rolled the ball out to Sparky, who neatly evaded his marker and passed to Whizzer — who whizzed down the wing and crossed the ball to Sam. She then controlled the ball superbly and dropped it in my path. In spite of being obstructed by that brute Ram I thumped the ball first time and it hit the back of the net with a satisfying sizzle. What a goal!

We went wild with delight. I think that was our undoing. Straight from the kick-off, Ram ran with the ball towards our goal. If he wasn't so interested in cheating, he would be a very good footballer, and he was really turning it on now. He glided past everybody until it was just me and Lump left. I knew he would go to my left so I stepped that way forcing him further out. He tapped the ball past me and made a run. There was no way he could get to the ball, but the next thing I knew he was rolling all over the floor in agony. I never touched him! Honest! But, blow me if the ref. didn't whistle and give him a penalty. Ram deserved an Oscar for his performance, I thought bitterly. As he got up, he smirked at me and winked. I could have kicked his teeth in! Trouble was, I tried to do just that. The referee didn't like it, pulled me over, and told me to clear off the pitch.

What injustice! I was so mad I couldn't contain myself. I gave that ref. a piece of my mind but it didn't help, I had to go! Sullenly and with the sympathy of the rest of the team, I sulked off.

From the side I watched as Ram scored from the penalty, and despite some marvellous efforts from the gang, Sam in particular, they ran out the winners 3-1. I was sick.

We got the award ceremony over with as quickly as possible and skulked off with the jeers and taunts of Ram's lot in our ears. I didn't know whether to be mad with myself for getting sent off or with the referee for letting Ram's lot get away with it, or mad at Ram's gang for cheating. So in the end I got mad with everybody and went off home to sulk.

Why is the whole world against me? What have I done to deserve all this? I felt really sorry for myself.

7

THE PIANO INCIDENT

Things couldn't get much worse. First we lost the club, then there was all the trouble over that crook Booth. The disaster of the march and the sit-in fiasco were bad enough. Now, there was the ultimate catastrophe — defeat in the five-a-sides by Ram's team. Life was getting grim!

The club evenings settled in to a pattern of being quite good, but occasionally spoilt by someone from the church wanting to use our room or complaining about the noise and mess. We hardly ever saw the Vicar. I think he must have been hiding somewhere!

Some weeks later, a stranger walked in to the club. We are a mixed bunch, with kids whose parents come from many different countries, but so far no one in the club had parents who came from India, even though there were some in my class at school. This kid wore a turban and was obviously very nervous of us all.

Doug must have met him before because he went straight over and said, 'Hello again, glad you could come.' Then he brought the kid over to us and introduced him. 'Hey everybody, this is Rajinder Singh Chopra, Raj for short, just moved on to the street.'

Sparky went up to him and said, 'Hi, come on over and have a game of darts.'

I thought I'd better make it clear to him where he stood, so I stopped them on their way to the dart-board and said stiffly, 'I'm Nick, the gang leader, hello.'

He looked at me warily and responded with a quiet 'Hello'. On first meeting he didn't seem to offer any competition so I left it at that, making a mental note to take him on at pool, just to put him in his place. As it was I had a good chance the next week to make my point. First I beat Sparky in a little pool competition we had arranged, so then I hammered Raj out of sight. I felt better after that.

I was getting fed up with club. Nothing much seemed to happen over the next week or so and life was very boring really. The church people were forever moaning about the mess and how rude we were. I told them where to put themselves a few times — I wasn't going to be called rude by anyone.

Then came the incident of the church piano. For as long as I can remember, that piano has sat around without being used much, so why there was all the fuss when 'it' happened, I don't know. Some adults really are unpredictable. I know I won't be like that when I'm old.

It was just an ordinary sort of evening, nothing very exciting. Some of the church members were in the kitchen preparing food and stuff for a bazaar. Aunty Edna was one of them and she and a couple of her mates kept slipping us the odd fairy cake. I'm a sucker for fairy cakes!

But to get back to the story. I've got a soft football which we used to play with in the club hut for all sorts of games. I had brought it along to the church hall, and Doug said we could use it, as long as we played 'gentle' games. He very firmly said that our

57

favourite game, passball, was out of the question because something would get damaged. So we had to wait till he was out of the room before we could put in a quick game.

Passball involved splitting into two teams of four, with one person standing on a chair at each end of the room. The ball was passed around the team until it reached your mate standing on the chair, and that was one point. The only rule was that you couldn't move your feet when holding the ball. Quite a harmless game really. In the old hut we had been allowed to use furniture to gain extra height, and that, together with the speed we threw the ball, caused Doug to ban it.

The night of the 'incident' in question I was just dying for a game of passball. Luckily Doug had to help organize something outside for the bazaar so he put us on our honour to behave. I ask you! The moment he was out of the room, I produced the ball which I had hidden behind a chair for just such an occasion and called out, 'Who's for passball, then?'

'Great,' replied Sam, quickly volunteering with Whizzer who was always ready for some action. Lump absolutely refused to stir himself — just sat there eating crisps as usual. Chip was persuaded but wasn't that keen. We were still one short to play against five of the club regulars not in my gang.

I looked around for another player. Then Raj came up to me and said, 'I'd like to play, if I may.' I wasn't sure about this. Ever since Raj turned up he had been trying to get in on the gang and I couldn't sort out why. I am always suspicious of people until I really know them — most can't be trusted, they only want something from you, or at least that's how it seems to me. But this was an urgent need and he was quite good at ball games, so I gave in, just this once. 'OK, Raj,' I said, then added quickly, 'but don't get any ideas, it doesn't make you a member of the gang.'

We began quickly and the game got noisier and noisier. At one stage somebody came out of the kitchen and told us we were making too much noise. It was lucky that no one was climbing on the furniture at that moment and Whizzer quickly hid the ball behind his back. As soon as they had gone we carried on at an even more frantic pace than before.

Now, when I play games I have to take them seriously. I can't bear just to play and not mind who wins. As far as I'm concerned, everything is a competition, and I'm going to win it, or there'll be trouble. (That doesn't count for school-work, of course. That's different — boring!) If I lose at anything I am cross for ages, like with the five-a-sides. Mum says that I'm just like my dad, which is strange because he's always telling me off for taking games too seriously. Last week for example, he clouted me for shouting at Mum when she messed up our family game of cricket on the park. I bet he did it when he was my age.

But, back to the story. The game of passball was getting more and more heated. I couldn't get past Stewart, a tall guy on the other side, so I decided to resort to using the furniture to get higher.

Out of the corner of my eye I saw the upright piano, and its stool. I made a dash for it, put one foot on the keys, making an awful noise, put the other on the top of the piano and hoisted myself up. It was harder than I thought to keep my balance up there because I got a surprise. Half of the top was open, but I made it and called out for the ball. 'Raj, pass the ball, quick,' I yelled.

Just at that moment Mr Marchbank walked in. He was a retired teacher and always looked very correct, wearing a smart blue suit with a white handkerchief in the top pocket. He was rather fussy and a real stick-in-the-mud. It just so happened that this particular evening he had decided to pop down to the church hall to see how the organization of the bazaar was going on. And I bet he wanted to check on us, because he didn't really approve of us messing up his beloved church hall.

Anyway, as I said, just as I was about to receive the ball from Raj, Mr Marchbank arrived at the door.

'Stop,' he ordered loudly. It was the worst thing he could have done.

Raj had thrown the ball hard because he was trying to impress. I turned in the direction of the shout to see what was going on. I began to overbalance and wobble a bit. When the ball arrived at my head, it put the finishing touches to my wobbling act. Everyone was looking at me. There were gasps of horror as they watched me wobble — to the left, then the right, then back again. Eventually, after what seemed like an age, one foot slipped right down into the piano and the other crashed down on the keys. The crunching and cracking was horrific.

A huge silence fell upon the hall and I just stood there — with one leg in the piano and one out. Nobody moved as I extricated myself and sat on the piano-stool rubbing my leg. But the silence didn't last long.

'You blithering idiot! Look what you've done

now,' yelled Mr Marchbank, advancing across the hall towards me.

'Nick, are you all right?' shouted Sam, dashing to my side.

Doug came rushing in after hearing all the commotion. 'What's happening? What have you done now?' he demanded.

Out from the kitchen rushed several old ladies. 'Oh dear, oh dear, whatever is going on?' they clucked.

There I sat but everybody was looking at the piano, except Sam, who was studiously dabbing my leg with her hanky.

'I knew we should never have let you lot in here,' went on Mr Marchbank. 'You're all nothing but trouble. You have no respect for property.'

But then good old Aunty Edna and her pals took up my defence. 'Now just you calm down Mr Marchbank,' said Edna. 'Just remember, these are perfectly normal children who have to let off steam. I'm sure Nick didn't mean to damage the piano.'

'That's not the point,' replied stuffy Mr Marchbank.

The gang and I followed this conversation like spectators at a tennis match, our heads moving from side to side.

'The point is,' replied Aunty Edna, 'that I remember *you* when you had a snotty nose and holes in your trousers, instead of a posh blue suit and white handkerchief. I also remember you getting up to all sorts of mischief. What would have happened if you had been banned from the church hall, I wonder! Do you want these children to learn about Christianity and God's love for sinners, or do you want a tidy church with no people?' She was

61

marvellous. I felt like getting up and clapping.

'That's all well and good, Edna,' Mr Marchbank replied. 'But at this rate we'll have no hall left for anybody. I am going to report this to the church meeting.'

Doug turned to me and quietly said, 'I think you had better go.'

I wanted to join in the battle but decided this wasn't the best time. While everybody was still arguing, I slipped out of the door and was away. I wandered down the street aimlessly and sat on the wall opposite where our old club hut had been. There was nothing left and there was now an ugly corrugated iron fence with barbed wire on the top blocking my view. Old Booth had gone a bit overboard on security. I just sat there all on my own, feeling pretty low. No one seemed to care, understand or appreciate me. All everybody wanted to do was change me. Why couldn't they accept me as *me*!

As I was mooching about and looking at nothing in particular, I noticed the gates of Mr Booth's garage opening and a couple of shifty looking men appeared. They looked up and down the street, not noticing me, then waved to someone inside. From inside the yard a breakdown vehicle appeared with a car on it. One of the men leapt into the passenger seat and it set off at speed in the twilight. The other man quickly banged the gates to and I heard padlocks being snapped together. It seemed a funny carry-on to me! Why such secrecy about taking a car out of the garage? That shark Booth had always seemed a shifty person to me. Now I was even more convinced he was up to no good.

I wandered over to the iron fence and tried to find

a peephole to look through. There wasn't one. Somebody had very carefully made the whole wall completely secure without one tiny crack.

It was then that I decided something had to be done! It was no use telling my dad or Doug, they just wouldn't believe me after all the recent aggravation. I didn't want to get the gang involved in any more trouble. This time I had to do something myself, on my own. I decided the only thing to do was to investigate the garage and see what I could find out. My mind was made up. Next I had to plan how to do it.

I wandered off down the road home. In my mind I could picture finding a hoard of stolen jewelry, getting a reward, rebuilding the club, being interviewed on television as a hero.

Fame and fortune beckoned!

8

MIDNIGHT RAID

I lay on my bed 'planning the job'. I had always known that watching all those old 'cops and robbers' movies on the TV would come in useful some time — much more valuable than silly homework. From my background knowledge I figured out that I needed to 'case the joint' and also get together some tools for the break-in. Most importantly, I needed a torch.

On my wanderings about cupboards and boxes in search of the elusive torch I unfortunately drew the interest of Mo. At first I fobbed her off with, 'Just looking for something', but that didn't work for long. Then, worse luck, she noticed my prize, which I had found in a box of old toys.

'Why do you want a torch in the middle of summer when it's not dark?'

'Mind your own business,' I replied bluntly.

She followed me back into my bedroom. I could see her suspicions had been aroused. Sisters!

'If you don't tell me what you're doing, I'll go straight to Dad,' she whined. Seven is such a difficult age, and if little Mo didn't watch herself she would never make eight.

'I've got something to do, that's all,' I muttered.

She wouldn't let go. 'You tell me what or I'll go and tell Dad,' she said.

There was no way round it. I was going to have to

tell her. 'All right then,' I said, trying to make it sound as serious as possible. 'If you promise not to say a word to Mum or Dad, on pain of getting your arm twisted and being banned from all gang meetings for ever more.'

'I promise, cross my heart and hope to die,' she replied. She was a real tell-tale but I could usually trust her with important things. Anyway, it seemed a good idea that somebody should know where I was in case of accident. They never seem to think about that in films.

I began with great drama. 'I have seen something fishy going on at Booth's garage, I think he's up to no good and I'm going to investigate,' I said, whispering and looking mysterious.

Mo looked horrified. 'You mustn't get into more trouble, Nick. Dad'll kill you,' she said with wide-eyed concern. 'Why don't you tell Dad and let him sort it out?'

'What good would that do?' I replied gruffly. 'Do you seriously think he would believe me, after all the other disasters?'

'You must be crazy to do it,' she said.

I wasn't in a mood to listen to her. Nobody was on my side. I was on my own, now. I wasn't going to give up and be defeated. I turned on her, 'You keep your mouth shut like you promised, and leave me alone.'

She shrugged her shoulders and left me to get on with sorting things out.

Once again on the stroke of midnight I set off on my favourite escape route. Carefully I eased myself out of the bedroom window, over the flat kitchen roof, then down and along the top of the garden wall. Gently I dropped from the wall at its end, into the back alley.

Then I got the shock of my life. A torch flicked on and I gasped in surprise.

'It's only me,' came a voice I immediately recognized.

'Sam,' I whispered gruffly, 'what on earth are you doing here? And keep your voice down.'

'Little Mo told me all about it,' she whispered, 'and I wasn't going to let you go through with this on your own.'

I could have crowned that stupid little sister of mine! And, what's more, I was getting a bit fed up with Sam's constant attention. But by then I was quite glad she was there because I was beginning to feel just a tiny bit scared. Of course, I didn't say so. I decided to let her stay. Mind you, I didn't have much choice.

'OK,' I said, trying to sound annoyed while whispering, 'but switch that blinking torch off before you wake everybody on the street.'

'Oh, sorry,' she said, and we were immediately plunged into blackness as she flicked the switch. 'Now what?'

'Pick up that crate behind you,' I grunted, 'and follow me.' During the day I had placed the crate ready for a direct assault on the wall of Booth's garage.

'What crate?' asked Sam. 'Owww!' she squeaked, as she turned and tumbled straight over it. There was a terrible clatter as the crate knocked into a dustbin which then fell over. In the still night air the sound seemed to echo for ever. I clapped my hand over Sam's mouth as the window of my parent's bedroom opened and a shaft of light streamed out. The outline of Dad's head and shoulders lit by moonlight was framed in the open window.

'I thought I heard a noise,' he said. 'Better go and see what it is.'

In moments of panic, inspiration strikes. 'Meeow,' I whined, doing my best to imitate the local 'Tom'.

There was a pause which seemed to last forever, then Dad said, 'Good grief! It's that blinking cat from down the street again. I shall have some strong words to say to its owner.' From inside the bedroom I heard a muffled, 'Come back to bed, love, and shut the window.' The window banged shut and all went dark again.

Only then did I remove my hand from Sam's mouth. She gasped for air. 'There was no need to do it so hard,' she complained, rubbing her mouth as well as her shin. Women! There was no point in making a big fuss, so I picked up the crate and muttered, 'Are you coming or not?' and walked off.

We set off down the dark alley, then made our way onto the street, and made for the garage, carefully avoiding the direct light from the street lamps. There was a place where the new corrugated iron wall turned at right angles to run alongside the church. Here it was in shadow and we wouldn't be seen. I put the box down and turned to Sam. 'Wait here and stand guard,' I said, 'and whistle when anybody comes along.'

She nodded, said 'Good Luck' and watched as I placed the box against the fence. Armed with a pair of wire-cutters 'borrowed' from my Dad's toolbox, I stepped up to attack the barbed wire on top. I hadn't guessed the height of the fence accurately, and it was all I could do to reach up and cut. How I was going to get over, I had no idea.

When I had cleared as much as possible I made my first attempt. There seemed to be only one way. I had to get my hands on the top of the fence where there was a horizontal piece of wood and then I had to leap up and pull myself up the rest of the way. The trouble was, when I jumped against the fence it made a sound like a big base drum, so I had to stop. I needed more height.

I persuaded Sam to kneel on the box. She wasn't keen, but if she wanted to be number two in my gang, she had to learn to take the rough with the smooth. She knelt down very reluctantly and I carefully climbed up on her back, then eased myself on to the top of the fence. But there was more trouble. In my haste, I hadn't cut away enough wire, and I now found myself stuck by the seat of my trousers to a particularly sharp piece of barbed wire. It was difficult to know what to do. It was hurting anyway but if I moved it would probably hurt even more. I flashed my torch quickly down on the garage side of the ground and found it was clear. I foolishly made an instant decision.

'Decisions made in haste are repented at leisure,' my grandmother always used to say. She was right! I thudded to the ground and felt a searing pain in my right foot to add to the sharp pain in my bottom from the barbed wire. Stifling a groan, I sorted myself out and looked around. From the other side of the fence I heard Sam calling quietly but anxiously, 'Are you all right, Nick?'

Bravely I replied, 'Yes, now get out of sight.' I then turned my mind to the task ahead. My foot was sore but bearable and my trousers had a nasty tear which my mum wouldn't be pleased about. But now I was here, I was determined to go on. Besides, I had suddenly realized the great weakness in my plan — I hadn't worked out a getaway route! I looked around. In the dim light I could see lots of old cars littering the grassy area where we used to play. Over where the club hut used to be, was a new shed like a large garage. I made my way over and crawled around trying to find a way in.

On one side of the shed there was a small window that didn't seem to fit very well. I carefully eased it open. It was easy to climb through and I found myself standing in the pitch dark of the garage interior. I flicked on my torch and played it around. Over the other side was a workbench and I wandered over to see what was on it. There's one unfortunate thing about torches — they only light a narrow area and a clumsy character like me needs all-round vision. My left foot, in the dark, hit against something and there was a dull clunk.

I shone the torch down to see what I had kicked over. Trust me — it was a pot of red paint! Not a large pot, but big enough to spatter all over my shoe. Torn trousers, paint-covered shoe, Mum really would be pleased! I picked up a rag and dabbed at the paint, and managed to get the worst off.

I went on over to the bench. It wasn't loaded with stuff but there were a few blank pieces of metal that number-plates are made of, and lots of loose letters strewn around. At one end were small pots of paint, templates and stickers, used for decorating cars with stripes and such like.

I was just nosing around these, when I heard a low whistle from Sam, then the sound of voices from outside. Quickly, I flashed the torch on to some large boxes and moved to hide behind them. I was just in time!

First of all the lights went on in the yard outside, and I heard someone moving around. Then the door of the shed was opened, the lights were turned on, and, through a gap between two boxes, I could see the huge body of the Hulk framed in the doorway.

He looked around and wandered over to the bench, then back to the door. I breathed a sigh of relief. He hadn't found me! He was just about to switch off the light when he suddenly noticed the spilt tin of paint and a trail of red footprints. I watched in horror as he followed them — first to the bench and then straight for me. 'Ah,' he grunted, as he followed them. He called out over his shoulder, 'Boss! Over here! I think I've found something.'

Now was the time for decisive action. Just as he reached me, I gave an almighty shove and pushed the whole pile of boxes over on to him. He yelped in surprise, and fell over. I made a dash for the door and escaped out into the grassed area, now floodlit, where the old cars were parked.

Running as fast as I could with an injured foot and torn trousers I made for the spot where the barbed wire was cut and leaped at the fence. My fingers caught on the top, but I just hadn't got the strength to pull myself up. I turned and saw the Hulk appearing from the shed, and Mr Booth from the direction of the main garage. It was no good, I was cornered!

They ran over to me and grabbed me. 'Right, I've got you now, you little squirt,' leered Mr Booth.

'You touch me and I'll tell my dad,' I replied, frightened by his manner.

'How's he going to know?' he said menacingly.

Just then, Sam called from over the fence, 'Are you all right, Nick? What's going on?'

'Oh, there are more of you, are there?' said Mr Booth, startled by the voice. He turned to the Hulk and ordered him to go and catch the little blighters, as he put it. There was something in the way he spoke that really frightened me, and I called out to Sam, so she could go and tell my dad. Mr Booth's tone changed abruptly, and just as the Hulk reached the main garage to chase Sam, he yelled at him to ring for the police instead. He then manhandled me in the direction of his office. I knew I was in for big trouble this time, but was really relieved that Sam had gone to fetch my dad.

The police car arrived at the same time as Dad did. He didn't make a lot of fuss, but quickly got me into the police car and took me down to the station. I made a statement there, then Dad and I were taken home. I could see that he was livid, but all he said was, 'Why on earth did you do it?'

He didn't seem to listen when I told him about my suspicions of Mr Booth. He just sent me straight to bed.

I couldn't sleep that night. I was in big trouble this time. I felt sick and alone, everybody against me. Why wasn't anybody on my side?

9

◇

SPARKY TO THE RESCUE

The next few days were awful. Mum and Dad were very upset and kept shouting at each other. Dad was livid with me, and I was kept in my room and not allowed to play out. He also finally said I couldn't have the dog for my birthday. I hated being locked away like that — it was really depressing. Mo came in to keep me company, but that wasn't much fun because she kept giving me bits of news that I didn't really want to hear.

She told me that Sam was in a lot of trouble with her parents, and was very upset, crying a lot. I knew I should never have let her follow me, but what could I do? Mo also was the first to tell me that Mr Booth was definitely going to prosecute. The whole thing was getting too much, and I was really cheesed off.

I lay on my bed flicking mindlessly through a stack of old comics without any real interest, when there was a knock on the door. A head appeared. It was Sparky. 'Can I come in?' he said.

Why on earth was he here? A few days ago I would have said something rude and turfed him out, but at least he was somebody to talk to. 'What do you want?' I grumbled. 'Come to gloat?'

He didn't respond but sat down on the edge of my bed and fiddled with the edge of a comic. 'Your dad's pretty mad with you,' he began.

'Tell me something new,' I grunted.

'And you've really set Mr Booth against you,' he continued.

This conversation I didn't need. 'Look,' I said to him, 'I don't need to be told about all the rotten things that have happened or are going to happen to me. Also, I don't want a sermon from you. If you've come here hoping to "convert" me, you can forget it. I'll fight my way back. Nobody's going to beat me!' I had a lot of pent-up anger to get rid of.

I stopped. For a long time Sparky didn't say anything, just kept fumbling with a comic. Eventually he spoke. 'You know,' he began, 'you've got it all wrong. I know things have changed in the last year. I know I've changed. I made a new start when I became a Christian. I believe in Jesus Christ and that he died for me. And that he's alive today. I believe it's true, and it's changed the way I look at things. But all that doesn't mean we can't still be friends.'

When he started to talk about being a Christian it made me squirm with embarrassment. I don't know why, but it did. How he still wanted to be a friend of mine after the way I had treated him was beyond me, but right now I needed a friend. 'OK,' I replied, 'but I don't want any of your religion bit. *I'm* in charge of my life, not anybody or anything else. Right?'

We shook hands on it, solemnly. Strange thing to do really, but that's what grown-ups do! We had been friends for so many years and I didn't like the awkwardness that had come between us. Now he had come more than halfway towards me so I was quite happy to give it a whirl, just so long as he kept off that Jesus Christ bit. I didn't want to be brainwashed by anybody.

We sat silently for a moment. Suddenly Sparky picked up a pillow and hurled it at me, then jumped on me and started tickling. He caught me by surprise, and I laughed so much I thought I was going to die. With my last bit of strength I threw him off on to the floor.

There's nothing like a good friendly fight to make you feel better. We pushed and pulled, punched and tickled until we were both absolutely exhausted, and lay on our backs on the floor. It was good to be friends again.

'You know,' Sparky said, staring at the ceiling, 'I agree with you about Mr Booth. There is something fishy about his operation.'

'Then why didn't you join in and help?' I complained.

'Remember,' he replied, 'I'm not going to break the law. There must be some honest way of dealing with this without doing something wrong.' I suppose he was right, and anyway I was too fed up to argue.

When he thought I'd had enough, Dad allowed me out again. He wasn't very friendly towards me, but I think he felt that I was too low to get into any more bother. He was right! I didn't want to go back to the club at the church, but Sparky came along and dragged me in. As soon as I got there I could sense that everything was a bit flat and quiet. Nobody was leaping around, not even Whizzer. The gang came over to say hello when they saw me, but it wasn't with the usual enthusiasm. Sam in particular was very quiet and hardly looked at me. They weren't nasty or anything like that, but I felt like a failed David who'd gone to face Goliath with a sling and stones, then had to go back to the troops and say, 'Sorry, I missed!'

Sparky was being a real pal to me, and played me at pool. Whizzer bought me a drink, Chip some sweets and Lump even offered me a crisp! What a sacrifice! Inside I was feeling really guilty about all the trouble I'd got them into, but I didn't show it.

I had to leave the club to get back home early, as my Dad insisted. Sparky came along as well, just to keep me company, he said. As we made our way down the street, we talked about things that had happened with the gang in the past, and had a real laugh at all the memories. We didn't notice a couple of figures standing in a doorway, until we were up to them.

'Well, if it isn't our local neighbourhood thief,' came a voice. 'A very suitable name — Nick — isn't it?'

It was that swine Ram and his mate. I spun on my heels to face him. Talk about the pot calling the kettle black! I hated Ram. He'd never caused me anything but trouble. For years we had fought over who was top man in our area. We each had our own patch but always wanted to gain ground, to take over each other's territory. Now was the time for Ram to make a challenge, just when I was down.

I could have wished for a better moment, with Sparky so unwilling to fight. But I refused to give in — I'd do it all myself if I had to.

'Did you enjoy your defeat at football?' Ram asked, with a sneer. 'Mind you, with a girl in your team what can you expect? Was it just one girl or should the whole team have been wearing skirts, I ask myself.'

'You pig,' I said. 'You cheated and fouled to win.'

'You were the one who was sent off, not me,' he cut in. He came a step closer. 'Besides,' he said, 'I don't have "foreigners" in my team. If you take in immigrants and have to make your gang up with "them", your team's bound to suffer.' I knew how Ram treated the black children at school. It made me mad!

I was just about to say something when Sparky cut in. 'You know perfectly well that they're not immigrants. Anyway, Whizzer and Chip were born in this country. Besides, the colour of their skin doesn't matter, it's what's inside that counts.'

'Well, well, well,' Ram turned on him, 'if it isn't old goody-two-shoes, the latest convert to the God Squad.' He turned again to me, 'You really have got some queer folk in your mob — religious nuts, girls and blacks!'

I could feel my blood beginning to rise. 'You can say what you like, you skunk,' I said, 'but every one of them is worth ten, or even twenty, of your rag-tag bunch of left-overs.'

'Who says?' Ram took a step towards me.

'I do,' I said, stepping closer to him.

'You gonna prove it?' he went on, coming closer still.

'Yea,' I grunted, taking one more step and trying to stand as tall as I could.

We were nose to nose and toe to toe. He pushed me in the chest so I pushed him back. He barged me with his shoulder so I did the same to him. I knew he was setting up to swing a punch at me and I was watching out for it.

Suddenly Sparky stepped between us, the idiot. He held out his arms and said, 'Hang on a minute!

This is a stupid way of settling things! I've got a better way.'

What was he playing at?

'Get out the way before you get hurt,' I shouted at him.

'Yea, push off, so I can flatten him for good,' said Ram. 'You'd do better to go off and pray for him — he'll need it.'

But he didn't. He just stood there. 'I've got an idea,' he said. 'What about a replay of the five-a-side to decide who's best?'

What was going on in Sparky's brainbox? We were bound to lose. There was a long silence. I looked at Ram, and he looked at me. He was obviously weighing up the chances of success. It didn't take him long.

'I like it, I like it,' he said. 'This boy talks sense. You don't stand a chance Nick Baker. When we've taken you apart you can finally crawl into a little hole and keep out of my way.'

There was no way out. I'd get Sparky later, but meanwhile a brave response was needed. 'Oh yea? We'll see about that. Next Saturday, two o'clock in the park, and we'll put to rights the way you cheated us out of the cup.'

I knew we didn't stand much chance, and wished Sparky had kept his mouth shut. It was because he wanted to stop me fighting Ram. I reckoned I stood more chance in a punch-up than in a football play-off. But I couldn't refuse the challenge!

Ram looked aggressively at me and jabbed me with his finger, 'Two o'clock Saturday. Be there.' He turned, gestured to his henchman and swaggered off down the street.

I turned on Sparky. 'You've done it again,' I

77

complained. 'We stand no chance at football. At least in a fight I might have got one over on him.'

'Calm down Nick,' he replied calmly. 'The way you are at the moment, Ram would have beaten you easily in a fight. And besides, that pal of his was standing by to make sure Ram won. You're not using your head.'

'I would have used my head, given half a chance — on his nose!'

'Listen,' Sparky said, 'it is possible to win without all that.' He paused, then continued, 'We've got a secret weapon.'

I was getting confused. Sparky was talking in riddles. 'What on earth are you talking about?' I grumbled.

'The latest addition to the club — and hopefully to the gang,' he said confidently.

I scowled. This sounded like something fishy going on behind my back.

'Raj,' he added.

'Look,' I butted in quickly, 'nobody's joining the gang without my say-so. That kid's been trying to wheedle his way in and I don't like it.'

'It's up to you,' Sparky said. 'I've not told him anything about being able to be a member of the gang, but I think you better realize something.'

'What's that?'

'Well, before Raj moved here, he played for his district team at football. I've watched him play. He's brilliant!'

I was stunned into silence. I didn't know what to say. What was I to do? Raj seemed all right, so why was I making it a problem for him to join the gang? It wasn't because of his colour — that never entered my head. When it boiled down to it I suppose what really bothered me was that it wasn't my idea and I hadn't been around to find these things out for myself. Maybe Sparky was right. It couldn't do any harm to watch Raj play, anyway.

'OK, then,' I said to him. 'We'll have a knock around and see what he's like. No promises, mind you.'

'Great,' Sparky replied.

We finished our journey home. I couldn't begin to explain all the thoughts rushing through my head. I was beginning to get used to the new Sparky, and he was a good friend. I was also realizing what an idiot I had been over the club hut — getting Sam involved and causing a lot of upset to other people. I hadn't been meaning to do all that. Just look at the mess I'd got us all into. I had only been trying to help.

10

IN THE DOCK

I woke up with that awful sinking feeling in the pit of my stomach. It was the day of my visit to the magistrates' court. We went there in Dad's car, in absolute silence. I felt really awful. During the week the solicitor had seen me and talked about what would happen. And Dad hadn't been exactly comforting. I looked out of the window as the streets and houses flashed by in a blur.

All I could do was concentrate on keeping my breakfast down.

We arrived at the courthouse and parked at the front. Then Dad turned to me and said, 'Just remember, keep your mouth shut unless asked to speak and then say as little as possible.' In silence we got out of the car and made our way between huge, blackened, stone arches, through some mahogany-framed glass doors and into a long corridor. We turned off this corridor and into a smaller passage where there was a long bench. Dad told me to sit down and went on to report to a little man behind a desk. Then he came and sat beside me. It was like waiting for the dentist, but worse. Our solicitor came bustling along in a dark suit and was carrying important-looking files and documents under his arm. He was very tall and had a severe look on his face.

'You know what you have to say, don't you?' he said.

I nodded. Then he and Dad walked off down the corridor talking. Dad came back and told me he was going in now and both he and the solicitor left me. It's difficult to know what to do in this situation so I looked at the man behind the desk and smiled. He scowled back at me then carried on with his work.

Then I tapped my feet on the floor and drummed my fingers on the bench. The man coughed loudly and looked at me crossly, so I stopped. If only it was all over! I stared at the floor and started to count the number of tiles under the bench.

Suddenly a door opened and a man in a black gown appeared, like Count Dracula. 'Are you Baker?' he hissed.

'Yes, sir,' I replied meekly.

'Follow me,' he whispered.

I followed him through the door and into a large room. He motioned me to sit down and I had a chance to look round. I had imagined something straight from a TV movie, complete with scowling judge and earnest jury. Instead the room resembled a small cinema with tip-up seats. Dracula showed me where to sit. I was on my own on a row of seats down the side. On my right was a little three-sided box, the witness-box. Facing the front and ahead of me was another row of seats with a table in front. It was empty except for my solicitor at one end and the police sergeant who took my statement at the other. They were facing a raised platform with a large table on it, behind which were three enormous chairs. In front of the platform there was a man at a desk with a funny little typewriter.

I felt strange. It was as if I wasn't really there but

watching it through a TV screen. But when I looked to my left I was jolted back to reality as I saw people I knew. There at the back sat my father. But what really surprised me was seeing Sparky and Doug. Why on earth were they there?

My stomach churned again and I felt quite sick. All of this was to do with me. What was going to happen? What an idiot I had been! I vowed I would never do anything like this again as long as I live. I even asked God for a bit of help, just quietly. I wonder why you always think of God at times like this?

Then a door in the corner of the room opened and the court usher, Count Dracula, came in. 'All stand,' he ordered. You could hear the squeaks and soft thuds of the tip-up seats as everyone got up. The three magistrates, all ladies, came into the room, and stood behind the desk on the raised platform. I felt the blood draining from my legs and my knees start to knock. The magistrates bowed slightly, then sat down and we all did the same.

The clerk turned to me, motioned me to stand and spoke. 'Is your name Nicholas Bartholomew Baker?' he asked.

'Yes,' I replied meekly.

'And do you live at 102 Church Street?'

'Yes sir,' I replied again, my mouth getting drier all the time.

He then carefully explained to me that I had been charged with 'breaking and entering' and asked me if I understood the charge. Then he asked me whether I pleaded guilty or not guilty. I paused, shuffling my feet from side to side, remembered Dad's instructions, and responded. 'Guilty,' I said quietly.

I was allowed to sit down then. I felt really

relieved. But in my state of nerves I had forgotten it was a tip-up seat and there was the inevitable crash as I landed on the floor. Boy! Did my bottom hurt and my face blush! I wished the floor would swallow me up.

Now it was the turn of the police sergeant. He got up and outlined what I had done. He made me sound worse than Al Capone. After he'd finished I was sure that the least I would get was ten years. Then the solicitor got up, said a few words and to my amazement called Doug to the witness stand. Doug came forward and as he passed me, he smiled and gave me a wink.

'I have known this boy for some considerable time,' he began, 'and although he is very impetuous and lively he has never shown any criminal tendencies. I have found him an enthusiastic member of the local youth club, friendly and never malicious. He is sometimes a little boisterous but I am convinced that, given the chance, he would never allow this to happen again, and I am willing to vouch for him to that effect if required.'

I could have kissed him! We were too embarrassed to look at each other when he passed me on his way back to his seat. Good old Doug. The solicitor finished things off, making me sound like a cross between Mother Theresa and the Pope. I couldn't believe my ears.

We all had to stand then, and the magistrates left the court. I slumped in my seat. They were out for about ten minutes but it felt like ten years. During that time I bit my lips, drummed my fingers on the bench, tapped my feet together — anything to take away the tension.

The magistrates returned and we went through all

the bowing and standing routine again. The bossy lady in the middle of the magistrates spoke. She asked me to stand up, then she looked me straight in the eye.

'Nicholas,' she said, 'you have been a very silly boy. The way you behaved was totally without reason and caused the owner of the garage some harrassment.' I lowered my eyes dutifully expecting the worst. Would it be Pentonville or Parkhurst Gaol? 'I understand that you were angry that the youth club had to close, but that was no justification for your behaviour. We have decided, bearing in mind the excellent character reference from Mr Jones, to dismiss your case with a caution. Should you do anything else and be brought back to court — any court — this will be remembered and will affect any future judgement. You would do well to listen to your friends. It seems they have far more common sense than you have.'

Without further comment she and the other magistrates stood and left.

I couldn't move. Relief washed over me and drained the last of my energy. Dad steered me out and sat me on a bench outside. Doug and Sparky came along and slapped me on the back. I didn't know what to say to them, and could only muster an embarrassed, dry-throated, 'Thanks'.

The journey home passed in much the same blur as the drive to the court, but now it was a blur of terrific relief. As soon as I got home I went straight to my room and lay down. I couldn't get Doug and Sparky out of my mind. When the chips were down, they were there — real loyal friends. It made me think. Perhaps I should try and do things differently. Maybe my way of doing things wasn't always right. I dunno, it was all beyond me. I still couldn't stomach that religious churchy bit, but I decided that things were going to be different now. I was going to try and change — like all the best criminals.

I put my new resolution into action straight away. My Mum got the biggest shock when I asked to do the washing-up. It was the same with making my bed and tidying my room. I secretly thought it was a waste of time because it only gets messed up again, but it pleased Mum. When Dad saw the new Nick in action he just looked suspicious and muttered darkly, 'He'll never keep it up.' I must admit that the same thought had occurred to me. All this 'being good' seemed absolutely impossible to maintain — how did Sparky manage it? He even managed to enjoy it! I was quite impressed with Sparky in fact, because when you tried it, you realized just how difficult it was, not a cop-out at all.

The first time back at the club was difficult. I didn't know what to say to Doug. He seemed to sense my difficulty and spoke first. 'Hi, Nick, good to see you,' he said. 'I hope you've got over things. What about a game of pool?' I nodded dumbly, thankful that I didn't have to make a big deal out of it all. The rest of the gang played it down too.

Over the pool table Doug said, 'You know, I think Mr Booth is up to no good, too. But we will have to find an honest and legal way of finding out about it.'

'Mm,' I agreed. I didn't really feel like being involved with Mr Booth again — not ever!

Later that week Doug called us together to tell us that the church had decided to close the club down. I wasn't surprised. The incident with the piano must have been the last straw. Trust me! But Doug told us that it had been a close vote in the church meeting. Many people — Aunty Edna included — thought closing us down was all wrong. When Doug broke the news I think everyone expected me to explode. But I didn't. That's not to say I wasn't angry inside, but I was learning that it's not always the answer. I was beginning to realize that there were Christians and 'Christians', and that not everyone was against us. Perhaps after a while they would have another vote and Aunty Edna and Doug's lot would win.

Doug had persuaded them to allow us to meet as a group for coffee every week, but I didn't really think much of that. I kept quiet, though. Then I got together with the gang and we decided to take over the hut at the bottom of Whizzer's garden as a proper gang base.

I was beginning to wonder how long I could keep up all this being good before I exploded!

11

THE ACCIDENT

Time continued to fly by in this long, hot summer of disasters. It wasn't long before I could feel the enthusiasm of 'trying to be good' fading. Doing the washing-up had to go — it sometimes looked worse after I'd done it! I was telling Sparky about my failings as we walked along the road after a visit to the park for a practice game of football.

'I hear Ram's telling everyone that they're going to beat us easily at football,' Sparky said. 'He's going to get quite a surprise.'

I didn't have Sparky's confidence in spite of having Raj in the team. Ram's lot were very mean and were capable of using all sorts of ways, fair or foul, to beat us. 'Don't get too confident,' I replied. 'You know what Ram's like.'

To tell the truth, I was very worried about the game. I knew my patience wouldn't last and that I would do something stupid when Ram started playing dirty.

'Have we got a referee?' asked Sparky.

'I suggested Doug,' I said. 'And Ram couldn't find anybody else, so he's doing it.' That at least was something in our favour. He would be fair and honest, and you couldn't ask for more than that.

As we walked along, I saw Aunty Edna across the street, going in the opposite direction to us, on her way to the shops. As usual we both gave her a wave, and she waved back, then we carried on with our chat. We were walking down the street discussing the match when a car turned the corner ahead of us and hurtled down the street at a ridiculous speed. It rushed past us and, before we could turn to follow it, we heard a sickening screech of brakes and a dull thud.

We looked back to see the car slewed across the road and a hunched figure lying there. The car door opened and a large man leaped out and ran off in the direction of Church Street. We ran towards the car and saw that the body lying in the road was Aunty Edna. As we reached her she tried to move, but she groaned and passed out. Sparky knelt by her side and started to help her while I rushed after the man running away.

I saw him disappear round the corner into Church Street but when I reached the same spot and looked up and down the road there was no one to be seen. All I could see was the small side gate to Mr Booth's garage swinging open on its hinges, which was very unusual. It was usually locked and bolted, worse than Fort Knox. I ran back to the scene of the accident convinced that the man who ran off must have been the Hulk, Booth's right-hand man. The size of the man, together with the open gate, was enough evidence for me.

I looked down at Aunty Edna. She was not moving and looked terribly white. I couldn't see any blood but she was lying awkwardly, with one of her legs and an arm in a strange position. Sparky was being very good; he had been to some first aid classes. He had told a woman from a nearby house to go and phone for the police and an ambulance, and was now trying to make Aunty Edna as comfortable as possible. Someone had brought a blanket and a pillow, which was carefully placed under her head. Sparky wouldn't allow anyone to move her and covered her with the blanket. Then we waited in an eerie, hushed silence.

Grown-ups are really strange! They all came rushing out of their houses when the accident happened, but most of them were quite useless. They just stood and stared like it was some sort of circus stunt, occasionally whispering to each other. Two of them came over and tried to do useless things, like sweeping the road around Edna. Sparky had to get very sharp with two other women who suggested we ought to try and lift her into a house. Another woman brought a cup of sweet tea — which was a bit daft because Edna was unconscious. Even I knew that you weren't supposed to do that! So we all just stood there, waiting.

One or two old ladies were saying, 'Oh dear, oh dear, oh dear,' and holding handkerchiefs to their mouths. Then, quite suddenly, Aunty Edna opened her eyes.

'It's all right, Aunty Edna. The ambulance will soon be here,' said Sparky soothingly.

She smiled weakly and gripped his hand. Boy, he was fantastic. I just stood around like a spare part. Then she winced with pain and passed out again. Sparky looked up at me. I obviously didn't look too good. 'Why don't you sit down Nick?' he said quietly.

I thought that was quite a good idea. I didn't want to seem soft, but that sort of thing always made me feel queasy. So I sat down before I fell down!

After ages, or so it seemed, we could hear the sound of the police and ambulance sirens coming closer. As they appeared round the corner of the street, the sound increased dramatically. They drew to a stop and everything flowed into a smooth efficient operation. Two burly policemen got out of the car and began to clear people away, setting up signs and plastic bollards. Meanwhile, one ambulanceman rushed to Aunty Edna's side and took over from Sparky, whilst the other opened the back of the vehicle.

After a quick look at Edna, the man with Sparky called for some straps and bandages from the ambulance. He then carefully straightened out her leg and strapped her legs together. He also fastened her arm across her chest with a broad bandage. Then both men got the stretcher out and carefully placed her on it. Quickly, they slid the stretcher into the vehicle, said something to the policeman, and were off in a flash of white and luminous yellow, blue lights flashing and siren blaring.

Meanwhile, another police car had arrived. This time it was a little patrol vehicle instead of the enormous red and white traffic Land Rover that came first. Out from the vehicle, placing his helmet steadily and carefully on his head as he walked, came Dad. Was I pleased to see him!

He looked at me and asked if I was all right. Sparky answered for me. 'A bit shaken I think,' he said.

Dad turned to Sparky and asked what had happened. 'This car knocked Aunty Edna down and the driver ran off,' Sparky replied.

'Did anyone else see it?' Dad asked.

'No, I don't think so.'

'OK. Go and sit in the car,' Dad said quietly to the two of us.

We did as we were told and Dad went to have a word with the two other policemen. Then he returned to us and got in the car.

'I'm taking you down to the station,' he said. 'You need to make a statement, and you look as if you could do with a strong cup of tea.' We didn't argue.

At the police station we sat in an interview room and Dad brought in some huge mugs of tea, then left us for a bit. When he returned, he half smiled, which was a real effort for Dad. 'For once,' he said, 'you appear to have done something right. The police at the scene said that you were marvellous, and did exactly the right thing.' He looked at us. 'Are you feeling OK now?' he asked.

We both nodded, beginning to relax.

'Right then,' he said. 'Tell me what happened.'

I was feeling a lot better and wanted to make sure that Dad clearly understood exactly who had done it. The thought of Aunty Edna lying in hospital made me very angry. She was a smashing old lady who would never hurt anybody.

'I know who did it,' I said bluntly.

'Oh?' asked Dad, startled.

'It was the Hulk, Mr Booth's assistant,' I continued. There was absolutely no doubt in my mind. I could see Dad's brow furrowing, and a hard look came in his eyes.

'How can you be so sure?' he said. 'Let's start at the beginning. Tell me all that happened.'

I began to recount everything; the screech of brakes; the man running away; the open gate.

Dad listened. Then, after a moment's pause, he turned to Sparky. 'What did you see?' he asked.

Sparky hadn't seen anything, because he had been concentrating on helping Aunty Edna.

'Don't you believe me?' I demanded, amazed that Dad hadn't rushed out to get a posse round to Booth's garage.

'Look,' he replied. 'You had a back view for a few seconds, and you saw an open gate. That's not enough evidence.' Sometimes my father is so *slow*. If he'd been on the Titanic he would still be checking for leaks as the ship went down, saying, 'We must be sure before we do anything, we must be s. . . glug, glug, glug!' Are all parents like this, I ask myself? Or just those who happen to be policemen as well?

'So you're going to do nothing about it?' I asked sharply.

'No,' he replied. 'The car was stolen but we don't know who by. Aunty Edna was badly hurt in the hit-and-run accident. It's all very serious and the CID will deal with it. But I'm not going to let you shoot your mouth off, just because you believe Mr Booth is the city's answer to "The Godfather". When you are interviewed in a minute or so, make sure that you stick to the evidence, not opinions! Remember the bother you are already in, and what that magistrate said.'

He left us, and I turned to Sparky. 'What do I do?' I asked despairingly.

'I think you should stick to the facts,' said Sparky. 'If you make a big thing of this you'll only get yourself into bother, and nobody will believe you.'

My mind ticked over with everything I had seen and the things that had been said. I kicked the table in frustration. But when the detective constable came in I stuck strictly to the evidence and not opinions. I hated myself for it. Honesty's a funny thing, I thought.

But I knew that I wasn't going to let the thing rest there. Not me!

12

❖

RETURN MATCH

Sparky and I sat on the kerb outside our houses flickering stones, waiting for Sam. I was still very bothered about Aunty Edna's accident and the way Dad had reacted.

'I know I go over the top sometimes, but I'm absolutely certain that the bloke who ran off was the Hulk,' I said.

'There's nothing you can do about it at the moment,' said Sparky.

'But do you *believe* me?' I demanded.

'I don't believe you'd tell a lie about it,' he replied. 'But you do sometimes get a bit carried away and let your imagination run riot.'

We fell silent while I thought about that. I was convinced that I hadn't imagined it, and the more I thought about it, I was convinced that Booth and the Hulk were involved somehow.

I flicked a few more stones out into the road. 'I'm sure it was him,' I continued. 'And I don't see why he should get away with it.'

'Well, if you're so convinced, you'll just have to be more patient and wait for some more evidence,' Sparky said.

'You mean another old lady knocked down?'

Sparky shrugged his shoulders. But I was like a dog with a bone and wouldn't let go. 'Why does God allow such things to happen anyway?' I demanded.

'Aunty Edna's a regular down at church, one of the best. Yet she's the one that gets knocked down by a crook. I doesn't seem fair or right to me, particularly when no one gets done for it. Where's God in all of this?'

Sparky was stumped at this flow of questions. I think I must have said out loud the same questions he was asking inside. He sat with his head in his hands and his brow furrowed. Then he said, 'I don't know, I just don't know. But I'm sure there must be an answer. After the match we'll go and ask Doug. He'll know the answers. We'll tell him about Booth and the Hulk as well, and see what he says.' This seemed a reasonable idea to me and anyway Sam appeared then and we had to get on with the arrangements for the match against Ram's lot.

We sat in the hut and began to chat about the game. The gang now included Raj. He was a very quiet lad, but very loyal and friendly, so I had let him join. Besides, he was a fantastic footballer!

Once again I was dreading the thought of Sam blowing a fuse. With Raj in the team we didn't really need her. How to break the news, that was the problem. I remembered the last time.

'Right,' I said. 'The team!'

'Chip, you play in goal,' I continued. As usual he wasn't keen — I could tell by the expression on his face — but he didn't argue. He knew it was useless.

'The four others,' I went on quickly, 'will be me, Sparky, Whizzer and Raj.'

There was an ominous silence.

'The reserve,' I concluded, 'will be Lump.' At this, mouths dropped open and everyone glanced at Sam. Tears of anger formed in her eyes, but she didn't say anything.

'I don't really want to play,' groaned Lump. 'I'm useless and I hate football. Besides, Sam is much better.'

I wish he had kept his mouth shut. I knew it wasn't a popular decision but I didn't want Ram to have the chance to give me a verbal going-over, and get Sam as well, all over again. 'No,' I said firmly, 'you're the reserve, Lump, and that's the end of it.'

'Why?' demanded Chip.

'Because this game is going to be rough and nasty and I don't think it would be fair on Sam,' I replied, getting annoyed. 'That's not the real reason,' butted in Sam sharply. 'You're just afraid of what Ram will say.'

She was right!

'Go on, let her play,' put in Whizzer.

I tried another tack. 'I'm only trying to protect her,' I said to him. It sounded really lame!

'I don't need protection,' she responded aggressively. 'I've proved it once and I can do it again.'

I could see I wasn't going to win, again, and gave in as graciously as I could. 'All right, then,' I said. 'Sam is reserve instead of Lump.'

Both Lump and Sam whooped in delight, for different reasons.

It was another warm and sunny day at the park. We were there early and kicked a ball around for practice. There were no special posts this time, no kits borrowed from school. I took along four sticks I had found in the shed and we banged those into the ground for posts. Fortunately all the markings from the tournament were still there, just visible.

Ram's lot came swaggering across the park to join

us, and at the same time Doug appeared on his motorbike. After parking and removing his helmet he began to get the game organized. We were all wearing an odd collection of tee-shirts and shorts. Doug looked around and asked, 'How am I going to sort out the teams? Nobody's wearing the same colour as anybody else.'

Ram leered across at Sam and then said to Doug, 'When we play at school one team takes off its shirts.'

Sam blushed. This was just the sort of thing I expected from Ram.

'Seeing as Nick has to play with girls in his team, we'll take off our shirts. Don't want to embarrass anyone, do we?' Ram said.

I could have strangled him, and knew that this was just the start. It could only get worse. I just hoped that Doug was up to it and wouldn't let Ram get away with things. We needed all the help we could get and Ram was extremely clever at cheating without being caught.

The match began and straight from the kick-off Ram and the rest of his mob set about barging, pushing and kicking — not the ball, but us!

After about five minutes what I had been dreading happened. Ram hit a fierce shot at our goal and Chip parried it. Ram then rushed in to get another kick at the ball, knocked Chip over, trod heavily on his fingers and hit the ball between the posts. He claimed a goal of course, but in spite of Ram's angry protests, Doug wouldn't allow it. Poor old Chip lay writhing on the ground, clutching his hand. It was obvious he couldn't go on. It was bad luck for Chip. Every time he played against this lot he got hurt. So, once again Sam had to come on. She was delighted. To my amazement she went straight up to Ram and said, 'Just you watch yourself, I'll get you for what you did to Chip.' Ram was too flabbergasted to reply.

We put Whizzer in goal and Sam took over Whizzer's place and the game went on. It was a pretty even match, with no one particularly on top. Towards half-time Ram must have said something to his team because they began to get very rough. I knew they were trying to get me going, and they nearly succeeded! Just before half-time they gained a goal using exactly the same trick as last time. Ram was coming past me, then dived as if I had pushed him. Doug blew the whistle and awarded a free kick and they scored. I was sick! There was no point in getting angry with Doug, he was doing his best and Ram was a master at this manoeuvre. But I was ready to stick one on Ram!

For some reason the half-time whistle went early, or so I thought. Sparky and Doug seemed to be chatting, then Doug gave Sparky a knowing nod as he blew the whistle. Sparky dragged me to the side.

'They're stringing you up again,' he said.

'I know, but I can't stop myself.'

'Don't be daft,' said Sparky. 'It's just what Ram wants. Think about it. What do you want most — to win the game, or to smack Ram in the mouth and watch us lose from the sidelines?'

There were merits both ways as far as I was concerned, but after some thought I said to Sparky, 'We have to win, I suppose.'

'Then control yourself,' he urged. Then he walked off.

The second half was worse than the first. Ram began to make nasty comments to the coloured lads in the team when he was near them but when Doug couldn't hear. They tried pushing Sam around but, judging by their bruised shins, she gave as good as she got. They were still trying to get me going as well, but with the help of occasional looks and digs in the ribs from Sparky, I managed to stay in control.

Raj was fantastic. He didn't say much, but boy, did he speak with his feet! And it was from one of his dazzling dribbling runs that our equalizer came and not a moment too soon. With two minutes to go he worked his way down the left and crossed the ball. In spite of some pushing and shoving, I forced my head round a defender and nodded the ball in. What a goal!

It was great to feel the satisfaction of having scored against that foul mob and seeing their heads drop. There was hardly time to start up again and so we finished with a one-all draw. Everything was to be decided on penalties. We each came up to try and in turn scored till four had gone from each team.

Now there was just Ram to shoot for them and Sam for us. Ram came up and placed the ball carefully. Doug blew the whistle and he shot. Like a dream Whizzer leapt athletically to his left and tipped the ball around the post. We all leapt on him with delight while Ram stood with head bowed and hands on hips.

It was all up to Sam now. After quietening us down and shutting Ram's lot up who were making remarks and trying to put her off, Doug went to the side of the goal. Sam came up and placed the ball carefully on the spot. She turned and looked at us. We clenched our fists in encouragement. The whistle went and after a short run she thumped the ball! It skidded past the sprawling goal-keeper, just inside the post. We were in ecstasy, rushing up and slapping Sam on the back. We had won! Totally forgetting myself, I gave her a hug and a kiss. Boy did I blush when I realized what I had done!

The game was over and we were triumphant. First, Doug cleared off Ram's lot who were making dark threats. Then we set off for home. As we left the park we were nearly run down by a car which was taking the corner much too fast. I could swear that it was the Hulk driving it. I looked at Doug and Sparky who looked back, thoughtfully. It had gone before we even thought of taking its number. None of us said anything, but I knew what we were all thinking.

That night I lay in bed thinking about the events of the day. I thought again about what a great pal Sparky was, and his brilliant idea for beating Ram. I wouldn't tell him to his face, but I was really impressed, and a bit envious of how he coped with the situation. What made me squirm was remembering the kiss I gave Sam. What had come over me? I blushed even now at the thought of it. As girls go she was pretty fantastic but, good grief, what would the others think? I just hoped she wouldn't get the wrong idea!

13

WHO DID IT?

It was Doug who suggested we should visit Aunty Edna in hospital. I wasn't very keen but Sparky talked me into it, reminding me of how she had stood up for me in the past. Personally, I would have preferred a game of football in the park. I found this 'doing good' thing a bit of a pain. Mind you, I knew it would give me a chance to ask her about the accident.

So there we were, waiting at the bus stop. Mum had made me bring a bunch of flowers which was horrible. I was having a real job hiding them under my jacket and all the front of my tee-shirt was wet. I wouldn't have been surprised if I had caught greenfly or something. I knew I would never live it down if anybody had seen me with them.

When we got on the bus I put them under the seat. Some idiot in the row behind kicked them, so by the time we met Doug outside the hospital they were looking a bit bedraggled. He took one look at them and one look at me, closed his eyes and sighed heavily. They weren't that bad! Grown-ups do tend to over-react. It was easier for Sparky — he had brought fruit.

Doug showed us the way. We pushed through the glass doors and went down a long corridor smelling of antiseptic and daffodils. Aunty Edna was in a little side-ward with three other ladies. She was lying in bed with one leg covered in plaster, strung up on a frame with weights. She also had one arm in plaster. It looked very uncomfortable but, as usual, she was smiling. When she saw us coming, she waved.

'Well, well, well,' she said, as we arrived. 'A visit by three handsome young men. This is my lucky day.'

Yuk, I thought. Why do old people say things like that?

'Hello, Aunty Edna,' Doug said. 'I thought you might like to see these two.'

'Oh yes!' she replied. Then, to our great embarrassment, she began relating to the other three ladies in the ward how we were the two boys she had been telling them about and how grateful she was and how wonderful we were. It was awful, but nice, both at the same time!

I dumped the flowers on her bed and sat down.

'Flowers and fruit, oh how lovely,' she said.

How quick can we get out of here, I thought. But there were one or two things I wanted to ask her before I went. I was determined to prove that the Hulk had done it.

'How are you?' Sparky asked her after a little pause.

'Oh, I'm all right, bless your heart, love,' she replied.

It went quiet again. It's always like this in hospitals — nobody quite knows what to say to each other, so you finish up asking useless things, eating all the grapes and staring at the person in the bed opposite.

'When do you think they'll let you out?' I asked.

'They said it'll be a while yet,' she said and for

once her smile slipped a little.

'Did you see the man in the car, Aunty Edna?' I asked bluntly.

Doug started and said, 'You shouldn't ask things like that, Nick. Not so soon after what Aunty Edna's gone through.'

'Sorry,' I said. But I did really want to know.

'Oh, I don't mind answering,' replied Edna. 'I didn't really see much, my dear. I do remember a very big man standing over me, dressed in black he was, then I passed out.'

That proved it as far as I was concerned. The Hulk always wore a big black jacket and black trousers, whatever the weather. It couldn't be anybody else. I shot a knowing look at Doug and Sparky, trying to make them understand from my face that I now had all the proof I needed.

'I'm sure the police will catch whoever did it before long,' put in Doug. He was trying to stop me asking any more questions. 'The car was stolen, you know.'

'Was it really?' she replied. 'Well, I never. I'm not angry at whoever did it, but the man has to be stopped from doing it to somebody else, so I hope he's caught quickly.'

Doug nodded.

Aunty Edna sat back. 'You know,' she said, 'I do feel very grateful for being here. I could very well have been finished off by that car. But I don't like seeing so many sad people lying in these beds. They don't see that they have anything to be happy about.'

'You're forgetting something, Aunty Edna,' Doug butted in.

'What's that, my dear?'

'Well, they don't think they have anything to hope for, that's why they're so sad.'

'Yes, you're right there,' Aunty Edna went on. 'Perhaps that's why God put me here. I can tell them all about how much he cares about them and wants to help them.'

This was beginning to develop into one of those uncomfortable conversations which I found very embarrassing, so I changed the subject. 'Anyway,' I said, 'Aunty Edna's just proved that it was the Hulk who did it.'

'How so?' asked Sparky.

'It's obvious,' I went on. 'She said that this guy that stood over her was big and dressed in black. There's only one man around here that fits a description like that! The Hulk in his black leather.'

'Come on, Nick,' Doug put in. 'Edna was half-conscious after being knocked down. No way is that anything like evidence.'

Aunty Edna was looking puzzled. I was just about to explain to her when Doug said quickly, 'Well, we must be going now. Come on, lads!' and hustled us out of the room. I think she was surprised to see us leave so quickly. I was annoyed. Maybe Doug was right and it wasn't enough evidence, but I was *sure* the Hulk was guilty.

We waited for the bus in silence. I kicked an old can in the gutter. But on the bus Doug turned to me all of a sudden and said, 'I think you might be on to something!'

This took me completely by surprise. I had just about given up hope. 'How do you mean?' I asked.

'Well,' he continued, 'bearing in mind all that you have said, added to the time that car nearly ran us over after the football game, as well as everything that's gone on in the past, I'm beginning to think it's very suspicious.'

'What are we going to do about it?' asked Sparky.

'Well, I think the only thing we can do is to go to Nick's Dad and tell him all that we know,' he replied.

I thought he must have finally flipped. Dad would never believe us! 'You can give it a try,' I said, 'but I would like to be some distance away when you do.'

'You've got your dad all wrong you know,' went on Doug. 'He's just concerned about you. He's a very good man and a good father. I'll speak to him. I'm sure he'll help.'

We shall see, I thought, but I didn't want to stand in the way of a just cause.

Doug was as good as his word. The next evening there was a knock on our door and there he was, asking to have a word with Dad.

'What's he done now?' asked Dad suspiciously.

'Charming,' I muttered under my breath.

'Nothing wrong,' reassured Doug. I could see Dad breathe a sigh of relief and he invited Doug in.

'You know,' continued Dad, 'Nick really owes you a lot after all that you said in the court, and I shall always be grateful.'

'There's no need to be,' said Doug. 'I only spoke the truth.'

'Ah, quite so,' replied Dad, flustered. 'What can I do for you then?'

'Well, it's about Aunty Edna's accident,' Doug continued.

'Oh?'

'I think Nick may be on to something.'

'Oh no!' said Dad. 'You're not joining in on this vendetta against Booth's garage, are you?'

'Well, I admit that Nick has gone over the top in the past,' Doug said, 'but I think it's more than that this time. Nick is convinced that it was Mr Booth's assistant that he saw running off. I've also seen him driving different cars around the neighbourhood, always far too fast.'

'It is a garage they run,' said Dad. 'What do you expect? They have to test cars after they've repaired them.'

At this point, I interrupted the conversation. I couldn't keep quiet. 'But they don't do car repairs. They can't! There was no equipment for car repairs when I was caught in there,' I said.

'Nick, I don't want to hear about that. It's caused enough trouble already,' said Dad.

There was a pause. 'However,' he continued, 'I hadn't realized that cars weren't repaired there. Look, I will speak to the Detective Sergeant on the case at the station tomorrow and see what he says. But you'd better be right about this.'

I looked at Doug and he looked at me. It was a step forward.

So it was that the next day I found myself at the garage, together with Doug, my Dad, and the Detective Sergeant, who made an appointment to see Mr Booth and the Hulk. (The Hulk did, in fact, have a proper name, but as far as I'm concerned, he was still the Hulk.) We all crammed into Booth's office. I had some bad memories of the last time I had been there, when Booth had been so nasty. He didn't look too pleased now.

'Well, what can I do for you?' asked Mr Booth sharply.

The Detective Sergeant spoke. 'We have been continuing our investigation,' he said, 'into the accident which occurred last week in the next street.'

'What's that got to do with me?' responded Booth testily.

'I want to ask your assistant something,' went on the Sergeant. 'Can you, or he, tell me where you both were on the day in question?'

'Yes,' Booth said shortly. 'But let me say first that I am absolutely fed up with people poking their noses into my business. That little monster over there and now his father and the church seem to be intent on putting me out of business. I'm going to make sure that the matter does not rest here. On the day in question,' he went on, 'we were delivering a car.'

'Can you prove that?' my father asked.

'May I suggest,' went on Booth, arrogantly now, 'that you ask your Chief Inspector how the second-hand car we provided for his son is doing. It was delivered on that day by us, and please thank him for the delicious tea he provided.'

There was a nasty silence. How could it be? It was impossible. My father looked at me and Doug. If looks could kill we would both be extremely dead.

'I see,' replied the Sergeant. 'I will, of course, be checking this up and will get back to you.'

'Do that,' said Mr Booth angrily. 'Now, I suggest you go!'

Without another word, we left! Doug and I looked very foolish and didn't say anything while the Sergeant spoke to Dad over by his police car. I could see that Dad was getting a right ticking-off — the back of his neck went all red!

The car drove off, and Dad turned. 'Thanks,' he said, sarcastically. 'That's just what I needed. It's the last time I listen to the local do-gooder and the terror of the neighbourhood.'

Doug decided on strategic withdrawal, made his apologies and left hastily. I was taken home — back to the bedroom! As I sat on my bed and stared at the wallpaper I thought to myself, 'If I spend any more time in this rotten bedroom, I shall go bananas!!'

Why do my ideas always go wrong?

14

ON THE TRAIL

With a lot of effort we had made the shed at the bottom of Whizzer's garden quite neat and tidy. His mum was happy because it had been a real mess before. We had scrounged some furniture and a bit of old carpet, and it all looked very cosy. I only hoped that there wouldn't be any visitors to our house which might mean Mum would go to get out the spare glasses from the front room cupboard. Orange juice didn't taste the same out of paper cups and the glasses really helped add a touch of class to our new den.

We were all sitting round enjoying the orange juice as I told them about the way Doug had persuaded my dad to get Mr Booth questioned and how it had all gone disastrously wrong.

'Doug must have been out of his tiny mind,' Lump chortled. Chip and Whizzer nodded in agreement and wonder. I think they all expected me to join in and say how stupid I thought he was. Well, they were wrong!

Through all the misery of the previous weeks I had learned a lot about loyalty and had found out who my real friends were. There was a lot about Doug that still had me puzzled, but there was also a lot about him that I had come to admire and wished I could be like that too.

'Just you shut your mouths,' I said to them

sharply. 'When the chips were down, he was the one that came and helped. I noticed you lot all managed to find something else to do! He's a good guy and you just better watch what you say or I'll thump you.'

Everything had gone very quiet. I thought it was because they were staggered at my defence of Doug. They sat there, their mouths open and eyes wide. Suddenly I realized they were looking straight past me. I turned, and there, standing in the open doorway, was Doug. I blushed like mad and felt sick with embarrassment. No one moved.

In the end, Sparky saved the day. He jumped to his feet and quickly changed the subject. 'I still think Mr Booth is up to something,' he said.

'Yes,' I added, finding my voice. 'Yes, it's still not changed my mind about him.'

'What do you think, Doug?' Sparky asked.

Doug stepped into the hut and looked around. 'I think you have made a fantastic job of this hut,' he replied. He sat down and said, 'And I also think that Mr Booth is not the innocent law-abiding citizen he claims to be.'

'What shall we do about it then?' asked Sam.

I kept the conversation going to get away from that very embarrassing moment when Doug had come in so unexpectedly. 'There must be something, but I'm not sure what,' I said. 'If I cause my Dad any more aggravation he'll lock me in my bedroom and throw away the key.'

'I've got an idea,' Sparky suddenly said. 'What about following them? I saw it work in one of those detective movies on TV once. It's called surveillance or something like that. Then, when we catch one of them breaking the law, we call the police.'

'That won't work,' grunted Chip. 'We can't follow more than one person unless we all split up, and if we do that, how could we let each other know if we find anyone?'

'I got a CB radio,' Whizzer butted in. He didn't ever say much, but reckoned to save it for something important. 'In fact I got lots of CB, my brothers and me,' he added.

'Great,' I said. 'What we'll do is this. We'll split into twos and wait at different spots covering most of the area around the church. When anyone sees anything suspicious, call the others up through me.'

Everyone was suddenly very excited, Doug included.

'I'll follow what's going on with the CB and come along in my car,' he added. 'I don't want anybody getting too involved in something they can't handle.'

'Just a minute,' cut in Sparky. 'Did you say *car*?'

Doug nodded, and held up a bunch of keys to prove it. We were amazed.

'Can we see it?' I asked, heading for the door.

We piled out on to the road, only to behold the biggest, ugliest, rustiest heap of old metal I have ever seen with wheels on. I could see that Doug was very proud of it, treating it like a new toy, but honestly it was terrible. It's funny how some grown men have this awful blind spot when it comes to cars. They just don't seem to see the rust or hear the awful engine. I have even heard my father talking to his car! I could hardly keep a straight face.

'Hey man, who paid you to take this heap of junk away?' Whizzer asked.

'Don't be cheeky,' Doug replied, obviously hurt.

We paced round it, prodding gently at the rotten

bodywork. Nobody had the heart to laugh, but there were a few cutting comments like Whizzer's flying about. Doug offered us a ride so we got in, hoping it wouldn't fall apart as Doug roared off on a short trip round the block. He screeched to a stop outside the hut and we fell out, a bit dizzy and travel-sick.

'Fair enough,' I concluded, nodding my head in amazement, then arranged for everybody to meet back at the hut at six o'clock.

That evening, after tea, we gathered at the hut and Whizzer handed out the CB sets. 'Don't break 'em,' he grunted, 'or my brothers will flatten me.'

'Right,' Doug said. 'Split off to where you're supposed to go.'

We broke up into pairs — Sam with Lump, Sparky with Raj, and Chip with me. We set off in our different directions, trying to look as casual and unconcerned as possible, and Doug settled down in his car.

Chip and I made our way down past the church and garage, and walked on down to the bottom end of the street. We ended up sitting in the entrance to an alley giving us a view along three different roads. Chip had brought a couple of his pocket computer games and we passed the time doing these. Every so often I called up the others on the CB.

'Bandit One to Bandit Two. Are you receiving me? Over,' I called.

'Bandit Two receiving loud and clear,' came the reply from Sparky. 'No contact yet, over.'

'Nor here, over and out,' I replied. This was repeated for Bandits Three and Four — Sam and Lump and Doug, that is.

Time really dragged and, apart from giving a

couple of girls from school a fright as they walked past, nothing much happened. I sat and thought about the last few weeks and how my attitude to Doug and Sparky had changed. It was good to be friends with them again. Sparky was such a great guy and lots of fun, and Doug talked a lot of sense, and I wished I could be like him. They both seemed to be having a much better time than me, and because they didn't get worked up so much, got a lot more done. The more I thought about it, the more muddled I became. It seemed the more I tried, the less I succeeded.

Then Chip nudged me and brought me back to the job in hand. 'This is boring,' he moaned. 'And I've got to go home soon.'

I must admit that I was ready to give up as well. Yet another good idea to bite the dust!

Suddenly the CB crackled into life. 'Bandit Three to Bandit One, Bandit Three to Bandit One. Are you receiving me? Over,' Sam was calling.

'Bandit One to Bandit Three, loud and clear, over,' I replied.

'We have contact, over,' she said with obvious excitement.

I nearly dropped the CB before I answered, forgetting the correct way of replying. 'Well, get out of sight and wait for me,' I said. 'Come on, Chip,' I called. 'Action.'

We raced off down the street until we reached the corner where Sam had been patrolling. I couldn't see her or Lump, but I saw the large bulk of the Hulk, sidling along trying car door handles. Fortunately he was walking away from us and we dived behind two cars. Sparky and Whizzer arrived a few seconds later and did the same. I saw Sam and Lump further on behind another car and motioned them to stay down and be quiet. As the Hulk walked on we occasionally ran on to another hiding place just like they do on TV when they are stalking criminals.

Suddenly the Hulk stopped, moved quickly to a very new estate car and dug in his pocket for something. I fell into a garden behind a bush and called Doug on the CB. He had a problem starting the car, which didn't surprise me. 'I'm on my way,' he replied to my urgent request.

I looked back at the Hulk who had now got into the car and was trying to get it started. The engine turned over and he set off down the street with a screech of tyres, just as Doug turned the corner behind us in his car, and screeched to a stop.

'Missed him!' I groaned.

'Never mind,' Doug replied. 'Pile in and we'll try and follow him.'

I opened the door and the gang fell into the back. I got in at the front with Doug. He thumped his foot down on the accelerator and we hurtled away.

'Do you think we'll find him?' Sam called from the back over the noise of the engine.

'We'll have a jolly good try,' shouted Doug.

I was a bit dubious about Doug's driving and also whether the thing would hold together under the strain, but he seemed confident. I was also glad not to be in the back, they were getting thrown about like dice in a pot. There was a wild look in Doug's eyes as he gripped the wheel tightly. I wasn't sure what would happen if and when we caught up with the Hulk.

I'd got another of my sinking feelings!

15

CHASE

Doug's old car rattled off down the road in pursuit of the Hulk, with us inside shaking around like peas in a pod. It wasn't too bad for me in the front passenger seat, but the others were suffering as Doug tried to keep up with the chase. The traffic in the city was very busy, but after a few minutes I saw the car about five vehicles ahead.

'They're up ahead, the blue estate car, that's him,' I yelled, shaking Doug's arm.

'OK, OK, but leave go or you'll have us on the pavement,' he yelled in reply.

'Don't let him get away,' Sam called from the back.

'I'm doing my best,' responded Doug.

We lurched in and out of the lines of cars and lorries, trying to keep within sight of the blue car. Poor Doug struggled to concentrate with the accompanying yells of 'There he is!'

'Don't lose him!'

'Left, turn left!'

'Round that lorry, you can do it.'

Doug's knuckles were white as he gripped the steering wheel and pumped on the accelerator and brake in turn. It was very hard to stay calm and at times I couldn't control my excitement, leaning out of the windows and yelling words of encouragement and abuse to people to get out of the way. The car seemed to be shaking itself apart as bits kept flying off, particularly as we took sharp bends. I hoped there was enough left on to keep up the chase to the end.

We managed to get into a reasonable position about two cars back, which was ideal for 'trailing', until we came to the Ring Road lights. The blue estate whipped through just as the lights were beginning to change. Doug tried very hard to get through but the car in front of us was turning right and blocked our way. We screeched to a halt and everyone was thrown forward.

'Ouch!'

'Ooo!'

'Gerroff!'

'My foot!'

'Ow!' came from close behind me. I looked at the heap of bodies trying to sort itself out, then turned to Doug. He was revving the engine and waiting for the lights to change. 'Go on,' I yelled, 'there's no one coming through the lights the other way.'

'I can't,' he replied. 'It's against the law!'

'If you don't, we'll lose him!' I shouted.

Fortunately the lights changed quickly. 'Go on,' I said again.

Suddenly he rammed his right foot down to the floor, pressing the accelerator to the maximum. We leapt forward, the engine screaming, and were past and away.

After changing quickly up through the gears Doug breathed a sigh of relief and looked at me. 'Don't get the idea I'm going to make a habit of this,' he said. What a guy! Straight up, he's really good. I had really got it wrong about him in the past. I wished I hadn't done and said the things about him that I had, but he didn't seem to mind. He'd forgiven and forgotten! Amazing! I wish I could be like that!

We raced on after the stolen car, and before long, with a shout from Sam in the back, we had caught up with it. Doug tried not to get too close so as not to give the game away. Now we were heading out of the city, the traffic was thinner and we had to drop further back. Soon we left the city altogether and were into the countryside. But there had still been no break, no chance to stop and ring the police. We followed the car off the main road and down narrow country lanes with steep banks blocking the view to either side.

It was really difficult for Doug. We had to be far enough back not to be noticed but not so far as to lose him. More than once we had to reverse at speed when we had missed a turning. I was totally lost now. We seemed to have gone miles and miles down narrow lanes at great speed. There was no time to check signposts and I never was any good at reading when my eyes are travelling upwards of seventy miles an hour.

Suddenly, we realized we had lost him. 'Where's he gone now?' yelled Doug. 'Look out for a turning.' We slowed right down and worked our way along between two high hedges looking for a turning.

'There!' pointed out Raj from the back, nearly knocking my nose off in his enthusiasm.

Through a gap in the hedge we could see the car driving down a track to a farm. Doug drove past the turn-in and drew to a halt further along.

'What do we do now?' grumbled Lump from the back in his usual unwilling way. 'Whatever it is, bags I don't have to leave this van.' What a coward!

The others groaned and chorused, 'Oh, shut up,'

in unison. However, Lump did have a point. I turned to Doug. 'What do we do now, Doug?' I asked. 'We're miles from a telephone, and if we leave, how do we know the car will be here when we get back?'

Doug thought a minute then replied. 'You and Sparky stay here under cover and keep watch,' he ordered. 'I'll drive on to find a phone box. If something happens, don't move, just watch and make a note of anything that will help the police.'

'They won't believe us!' I groaned.

'Maybe not,' replied Doug, 'but we haven't anything to lose.' Sparky and I got out.

Doug wound down the window. 'And remember,' he said, 'no heroics.'

Then, just as we turned to find a place to hide, two cars came hurtling out of the farm and screeched to a halt either side of Doug's van. Out poured six men. They wrenched open Doug's door, dragged him out, forced him against the side of the van and ordered the gang out. Nobody seemed to have noticed Sparky and me, but we were so shocked we didn't move. I came round quickly and nudged Sparky, pointing to the ditch behind us. The others were climbing out of the van and being pushed alongside Doug. They all looked very frightened. Sparky and I dropped into the ditch and scrambled through into the field behind.

We thought we had escaped because they hadn't noticed us, but just as we began to track along behind the hedge a voice from inside one of the cars called out. It was Booth!

'There's two getting away, through the hedge, over there,' he called. I would recognize that voice anywhere!

'Run for it,' I yelled to Sparky, and we hurtled at full tilt along the edge of the field, forgetting all thoughts of hiding.

'Split up,' Sparky called.

So I set off along the hedge whilst Sparky made across the field. I ran and ran. Turning, I saw Sparky making his way across the field with two men in pursuit. I hoped he would make it. I made it to the next field and carried on. Behind me I heard someone yell, 'Get him, he mustn't escape.'

'God, if there is one,' I said to myself looking upwards, 'please don't let anyone get hurt. And especially not Sparky.'

Suddenly, I was knocked sideways to the ground, and I felt a very heavy weight on me. I looked up into the ugly face of the Hulk, who had leapt on me from behind a hedge.

'Right, you little monster, I've got you, so you better come quietly or I'll break your nasty little arm off,' he grunted. He wrenched me up, thrust my arm up my back, and marched me in the direction of the farm.

'What're you going to do with us?' I demanded.

'I'm going to keep you here till the weekend,' he replied. 'By which time we will have finished our business here and be away. Until then you can be my guest in the little hotel round the back. Take him away, boys!'

'You'll never get away with it, my dad will be after us when he knows we're missing,' I retorted as I was dragged away.

'Oh yes I will,' Booth returned. 'Nobody knows where you are and out here we hardly ever see anybody.' He laughed and went into the farmhouse.

I was taken to an old barn. The doors were pulled

back. They threw me in and I fell in a heap of old straw. Before I had a chance to get up Sam was at my side. 'You all right?' she said.

'Yes,' I replied. 'Where is everybody? Is Sparky all right?'

'We're all OK,' came a voice. It was Doug.

Everybody was there. They were all looking a bit shocked, but nobody was hurt, thank goodness. Even though we were trapped it was good to be back with the rest of the gang.

'What are we going to do?' asked Chip, obviously frightened.

'Don't worry,' Doug said. 'It'll be all right.'

Somehow his calm voice settled everybody. I hoped he was right!

16

AMBUSH

Meanwhile, back at Church Street, the mystery of the missing gang gradually unfolded. I found out later, from Little Mo, what exactly happened on Church Street after our chase and capture.

As the evening went on, Chip's mum, as usual, was the first to get worried. She rang Sparky and Sam's house to see if he was there, but discovered that none of us were about. That set Sparky's mum thinking! She went round to check on my house, and of course, we weren't there either. At this point my Dad got involved and walked round to Lump's fish and chip shop, then on to Raj's home.

Finally, getting angrier and angrier, Dad went to the gang hut in Whizzer's back garden. By now, all our parents were very worried and Dad decided to give Doug a ring, but of course he didn't get any answer.

Just as he finished trying, Little Mo was brought downstairs because she had told Mum what we were up to. I had threatened her not to tell, but thankfully, in the end, she had talked. Mo told me that my dad was really anxious at this point. He decided to ring his friends in the force and see if they had noticed any of us. After drawing another blank, he contacted his station sergeant and told him what had happened.

A search was organized but Dad decided to go on

his own to ask Booth if he'd seen us. Of course, he found the place empty, but unlocked, and decided to have a look around. Inside he found licence plates and false registration documents just lying around — obviously people had left in a great hurry. He immediately rang the station and brought in the CID.

Then, just as he was coming out of the garage, he happened to bump into the vicar who told him that he had seen us all leap into Doug's car and hurtle off down the street at full speed. It was then that a full-scale search operation by the police swung into action. Of course we didn't know all this, but we were hoping for some miracle rescue as we sat it out in that cold, unwelcoming barn.

There was nothing we could do, but sit there, feeling rather cold, and wondering what to do. I got up and tried all around, looking for a way out, but the walls were made of breeze-block and the floor of concrete. There were a few bales of straw lying about which we used for sitting on. Sam suggested we pile these up against the roof and try to escape by knocking a hole through the corrugated iron. Chip pointed out, quite rightly, that this wouldn't work because there weren't enough bales of straw and anyway, when we tried to break through the metal, the noise would wake everyone up in the farmhouse.

'Well, I think we should just sit still and do everything that they tell us,' said Lump.

'You're just a coward,' retorted Sam.

'I know,' he replied quickly. 'I like it that way.'

'Oh come on, you lot,' Doug cut in. 'Arguing amongst ourselves isn't going to do any good at all.'

We all fell silent.

'What are we going to do?' I asked Doug eventually, after a long pause. I hoped he might have a magic answer!

'There's no point in rushing into something,' he said. 'If we do, someone is likely to get hurt. They're not going to hurt us if we stay quiet and be patient.'

I could see the sense in this and nobody else had any great ideas, so we made ourselves comfortable.

It wasn't long before we heard the sound of voices coming and the padlock on the outside being unlocked. Then the door banged open and in came a scruffy little man with a big tray of bread and cheese and a jug of water and some metal mugs. Behind him stood the Hulk, blocking the door. They said nothing, but backed out carefully. Then we heard the padlock and chain being put back in place.

'Great! Food!' Lump said as he made a bee-line for the tray. We all moved in quickly before he scoffed the lot and we disposed of all the simple provisions without any difficulty.

As I sat munching the cheese a germ of an idea began to grow in my mind. The only time that we had any chance of escape was when the food was brought in or the empties taken out. What had to be worked out was how to take advantage of this.

'Hey, everybody! I've got an idea,' I said enthusiastically.

'Oh no!' spluttered Lump through his cheese sandwich.

The rest didn't look particularly worked up either. I explained to them what I had in mind, how we needed to ambush our captors when they came back for the empties and then make a dash for it.

There was a long silence.

'Well. . .' I went on. I had been trying not to get

grumpy again, but the old me started to break out again, and I couldn't stop myself. 'Oh, come on,' I said impatiently. 'We've got to do something and no one's thought of anything better.'

'Well,' said Doug. 'It's rushing things a bit. We must be very careful. I have been thinking along similar lines myself. But we need time to plan it out.'

'That's the style, Doug,' I responded, pleased that at least someone was on my side. I knew he was still not sure about it, but I decided to ignore his doubts.

'Right,' I said. 'Let's get organized.'

'I've got an idea,' Sam suddenly said. 'Why don't we pile up the bales of hay to one side of the door and push them on to those thieves when they come in.'

'Great idea,' I replied. I like to see people getting on with things.

'Look,' said Doug, 'we mustn't rush into this. Let me think.' By this time everyone was busy piling up the bales. Doug turned to me, 'For safety's sake, let me take the risk. If you all make a lot of noise and cause as much confusion as possible, I'll make a run for it.'

'OK,' I replied. Doug was probably the fastest of all of us so he stood the best chance. I couldn't argue with that. So we all prepared ourselves, taking up the positions that Doug and I suggested. I knew that Doug was worried for us because he kept telling everybody to be careful and not do anything silly when the time came. Not knowing when anybody was going to come, we just had to wait, some more patiently than others.

I could see Doug quietly closing his eyes. I realized he must be praying. We could do with a few miracles in our position. Oh, how I wished my dad was by my side. He'd sort them out.

At last we heard someone coming.

'Right, everybody in position,' Doug said softly. 'And remember — be careful,' he added.

The key rattled in the padlock and the chain was slipped through its hasps. My stomach tensed and my hands were sweaty as they gripped the stave of wood I had found as a weapon.

Sparky was behind the straw, ready to push it all on top of them, and I stood opposite him ready with my stick. The rest of the gang and Doug were trying to look as natural as possible, which was difficult, especially for Lump whose knees were knocking so much I swear I could hear them.

The door opened and the scruffy little man came in with the Hulk close behind. Right on time Sparky did his work and the bales came tumbling down. At the same time I leapt out and hit the Hulk on his back, knocking him to the ground. Everybody dived into the scrum, trying to keep the men so confused that they couldn't do anything. Looking up, I saw Doug making his way out of the door, then I dived back in with renewed enthusiasm.

Fists were flying in all directions. Sam was biting away at one man's arm, Chip was kicking away at a trousered leg for all he was worth, and Lump just sat on the heap of writhing bodies looking like a great Buddha. With all the punching and fighting from the rest of us, we were very effective for a while.

Eventually, however, all the noise and shouting roused the rest of the criminals back at the house. Suddenly we were all pulled apart and thrown aside. The fight stopped as quickly as it had begun. I looked up, and there was Booth!

'Right,' he ordered. 'Get up, everybody. You lot, back against the wall.' Then he turned to the Hulk and the other little weasel, 'Some guards you are, letting a bunch of kids nearly get away.'

'Sorry, boss,' grunted the Hulk, getting up from the ground and dusting himself off. 'Er, boss,' he continued.

'Shut up,' went on Booth. 'And get this lot sorted out.'

'But, boss. . .'

'What, you idiot?' shouted Booth, very red-faced and angry.

'The vicar's not here,' mumbled the Hulk apologetically.

'Oh no!' yelled Booth. 'Well, don't just stand there, get off and find him! Don't let him get away.'

We were left in the barn, locked up again.

'I hope Doug will be all right,' said Sam quietly.

'Yes, me too,' I added ruefully.

We were all quiet, then. Thinking about Doug, about our homes, our families. Nothing seemed to happen for ages, and we just sat around. Occasionally we heard shouts, but the criminals didn't seem to be having any luck. Later, we didn't hear anything. It was night now. In that long silence, in the dark, we all waited with a little hope and a little fear in our hearts.

Suddenly, the door burst open and a body was thrown in. Booth appeared in the doorway with a lamp held up to his face. He looked evil. 'Don't try it again!' he snarled and slammed the door.

'Can we have a light, for a little while at least?' Sam called out.

The door reopened and Booth put the lamp just inside, 'For a little while,' he said. 'And no tricks.'

We rushed to Doug's side. He had blood on his head and was unconscious. After a while his eyes opened and he groaned, raising his hand to the cut on his head.

'Are you all right?' I asked anxiously.

He gripped my hand. 'I'm OK,' he said weakly. 'Need to sleep.' Then he closed his eyes.

I felt terrible. It was all my fault. If it hadn't been for my 'bright idea', Doug wouldn't have been hurt.

What had I done now?

17

ESCAPE!

The night was a long one, the silence broken only by the occasional groan from Doug. Our lamp had been taken away and they had thrown us a bandage so that we could patch him up. It was very difficult in the dark. Just like with Aunty Edna's accident, Sparky's first aid work came in handy again, and even with only a faint glimmer of moonlight through a small hole in the roof, he managed to bandage Doug's head very effectively.

'Is he going to be all right?' I asked Sparky.

'I think so,' he replied.

'No thanks to you,' remarked Sam aggressively. 'You really sold us another useless idea.'

'Come on, Sam,' cut in Sparky. 'There's no point in all that. Leave him alone.'

I slunk off to the back of the barn in the dark. There I sat, reminding myself of all the awful things I had done to Doug and others in the past and thinking about my lousy temper and how impossibly bigheaded I was. I heard someone coming over and saw the dark outline of Sparky. Feeling how I did, really fed up, I turned away and hunched myself up, staring at the wall. I couldn't face being told what I already knew about my own stupidity. He sat down and didn't say anything. He didn't need to!

After a while I couldn't stand the silence. I felt

absolutely terrible about what had happened. I turned to face Sparky, thankful that it was too dark to see his face, and he mine.

'All right,' I said, 'I was wrong. I've been wrong all along, so there's no need to tell me what I know already.'

'I wasn't going to,' he replied quietly.

'Oh!' That surprised me. I was silent for a while, then, 'Where do we go from here?' I asked quietly.

'I think,' Sparky replied, 'that we do what Doug wanted in the first place. We must be patient for the right moment, and not rush into anything that will hurt anybody else.'

'Mmm,' I said. Well, what else could I say?

'As for now, we rest and wait until it's light,' he concluded.

Totally depressed, I settled down to sleep as best I could.

In the light of early morning I woke up with a start to find Sparky and Sam at work comforting Doug, who was conscious, but looked very pale. We had surrounded him with bales of hay and covered him with coats to keep him as warm as possible. I held back. Nobody seemed to want to talk to me.

'What do we do now?' asked Whizzer of nobody in particular.

I said nothing, but Sparky called everybody together. I was so low and numb with depression that I didn't protest. After all, I wasn't such a good leader. Sparky suggested that we all pray for Doug and also to ask God for a way of escape. For once, praying seemed to be a good idea.

I sat back and quietly joined in as Sparky began to pray. Was it really true, as Sparky said, that God was always with you, and listening, and helping?

'Oh God,' he began, 'thank you for being with us here. Thank you for promising that you will help us if we ask. We ask you to make Doug better quickly and please help us to find a way to escape. Thank you for the help you're going to give. In Jesus' name, Amen!'

Nobody talked much after that. I was feeling a bit low and the others were either helping Doug or talking together. They didn't seem to want to talk to me. Sparky was messing about in a quiet corner of the barn.

'Hey look!' he suddenly yelled.

'What is it?' asked Sam impatiently.

'Look at this!' went on Sparky. 'I've found a loose brick.'

'What?' asked Whizzer. 'Where?'

'Over here,' he said, pointing to the area I had hastily passed by when looking round soon after we were thrown into the barn.

'Yes, look, it's a loose brick,' Raj added, joining Sparky. 'Let's loosen the others round it. One good shove will make quite a hole.'

'Why didn't we see it before?' grumbled Sam, 'it would have saved a lot of fuss.' Everybody went silent, and some looked at me. I went red and looked at the ground wishing I was invisible.

There was a long pause, then Sparky began to spark. 'I've got a plan,' he said, looking round at us all. 'What we do is this. We make up a dummy using straw and some of our clothes, then when they come in, we sit in a circle close together with the dummy turned away from them. They never look closely, only quickly count heads. That will give someone a chance to get right away without being missed, especially if we put back the bricks.'

I looked around and could see everyone thinking about this. I personally thought it was a great idea and wished I had thought of it myself. If only *I* had noticed the loose bricks. I also wanted to make sure I was the one to take the risk and make the escape.

'It's a great idea,' I said, stepping forward. 'But I want to be the one to make the break.'

Sparky thought about this for a bit, then replied. 'OK,' he said. 'I guess it has to be you. And it'll make you feel better as well,' he added bluntly. I didn't say anything, but he was right!

'But first,' Sparky went on, 'we must try the dummy idea out to see if it works.'

So we set to work. Sam looked after Doug while the rest of us loosened some hay and then sorted out clothes. We finished things off with Lump's scarf and Whizzer's bobble hat. From the back, with Whizzer on one side and Lump on the other, it looked very effective.

When the next meal-time came we tried it out. Two of them came in and dropped the food on the floor. I hid in the corner. They glanced round at the huddled group sitting around Doug, shrugged their shoulders and walked out. Magic! It worked!

'OK,' said Sparky. 'Success.'

'Yea, great,' added Sam. 'Which one is the dummy?'

'That one,' replied Whizzer, pointing at Lump.

Sparky turned to me. 'It's up to you now,' he said.

'Let's get on with it,' I replied enthusiastically. Underneath I was frightened rigid but I had to go through with it.

Just as I started to move the bricks, Sam ran over to me. She held my arm and put her lips close to my ear. 'Good luck,' she whispered. I blushed. For one moment, I had thought she was going to kiss me!

Sparky broke in on our romantic farewell. 'Take care, don't do anything daft,' he said.

I looked at him. He smiled, and so did I — it hid my terror. We turned and gently pushed at the brick. It fell back easily onto the earth outside and we soon had three others clear as well. There was just enough space for me to crawl through. I poked my head out and could see there was nobody round the back so I scrambled out.

'Push the bricks back,' Sparky called through the hole.

I pushed them all back into place, then turned to look for some cover. Just a little way off was a tractor. I ran and hid behind the large back wheel. From there I could see some of the criminals packing a lorry with things. They were obviously getting ready to move out so it was as well I hadn't waited until night-time when it would have been too late.

I waited there until I saw them stop work and go into the farmhouse. Seeing my chance, I ran for the fence, jumped straight over it, then ran along in the shadow of a hedge, away from the farm and towards the road. I was about halfway when I heard a shout from the farmhouse. Looking round, I saw someone leaning out of an upstairs window, pointing. I had been rumbled!

I turned and ran as fast as I could towards the road. I turned back once more to see if I was being followed, and ran straight into a tree. I hit my head and gashed my arm on a branch. A huge lump was coming up on my forehead and my arm was bleeding but there was no time to stop, so I carried on. I leaped through a hedge on to the road and looked round frantically for help. There was no one in sight!

Turning right, I ran along as fast as I could. The sides of the lane were lined with trees which gave me good cover, but there was still no one to help. By now I was feeling exhausted and couldn't go much further, so I stopped and leaned against a tree and slumped down, gasping for air.

I longed for a friendly car to come along and rescue me but all was silent except for the distant shouts from Booth's mob. Then I heard a vehicle approaching very fast. Without thinking, I ran into the road, ready to stop it. But something made me dive back into cover, just in time! From the trees I saw the car rushing past with the Hulk and another man looking out. I breathed a sigh of relief! That was close!

Then I heard another vehicle, much slower. It was a risk, but my arm was hurting more and my head was reeling. I had to take a chance! I jumped out onto the road and waved the approaching vehicle down with my good arm. It stopped. My stomach churned as I looked in, trying to see whether it was friend or foe. A man got out. I quickly realized from his perplexed look that he wasn't one of the criminals. He was in fact a farmer, taking his van full of produce to the market.

'What's up, lad? You all right?' he asked, looking at my arm and my head.

I tried to tell him what had happened and he put me in his van and we drove off to find a telephone box. I'm sure he hardly understood a word I said! Rounding a bend, we saw the other car ahead at the crossroads and the two men looking around.

'Climb into the back, lad,' the farmer said, 'and

hide among the boxes.' At the crossroads the Hulk waved us down, and the farmer opened the window.

'Not seen a lad about, have you?' asked the Hulk. 'Er, it's my nephew and I think he's lost.'

'Sorry,' replied the farmer. 'Don't see much down this road and certainly nothing this morning.'

He wound up the window and drove off steadily, trying not to give any clues that I was in the back. I looked out of the back window and saw with relief that they didn't seem suspicious. At the next phone box the farmer rang the police. It wasn't long before a white car came speeding towards us, blue light flashing.

It was fantastic! In the car was my dad, and I quickly told him everything. He called up the station on his radio telephone and passed on everything I had said. Then he turned back to me. 'Let me have a look at that arm,' he said. It was quite painful now, and it felt very bruised and sore. Dad bandaged it up using his car's first-aid kit. He looked at the huge bruise on my forehead and shook his head. 'I think you ought to see a doctor with that,' he said. 'Are you feeling OK?'

'Yes, I'm fine,' I said impatiently. 'Can we go to the farm now?'

'OK,' he agreed. 'I'd like to see that everyone's all right as well. But we must get you to a doctor before long.'

'I'm coming too,' added the farmer. He had never had a day like this before.

So Dad and I went in the police car and the farmer followed in his van. By the time we got to the farm the place had been surrounded and the police officers were rounding up Booth's mob. It was really good to see Booth, handcuffed, being pushed into a police van.

We got out and went over to the barn. Dad broke the lock and out came the gang. They were all in one piece, to my great relief. An ambulance had been called and Doug was carried into it on a stretcher. They insisted I went too. My head was really aching by then, so I didn't protest.

Before I went into the ambulance I had a quiet word with Sparky. 'Thanks for everything,' I said. 'You're a good pal, and I think I am just beginning to understand what you're on about.'

Sparky smiled, but he didn't say anything.

18

NICK & CO.

'Give me the ball,' I yelled.

Raj looked up as he heard my shout and passed the ball over Sam's head, to me, hurtling down the other pavement. I hit the ball hard on the run, and it thudded against Booth's garage door. Our goal was the garage entrance at the back of Mr Blake's butcher's shop, and so far it hadn't received a shot. The goalie, Lump, dived for cover when he saw me getting lined up to shoot. It was a very satisfying goal, and was greeted with shouts of glee from Chip and Raj, the rest of my team.

'You great lump, Lump,' groaned Sam at the unhappy goalie.

'Well,' retorted Lump, 'I hate football, I hate being in goal, and I hate being hit by one of Nick's piledrivers.'

It was just like the old days. It was half-time so we sat with our backs against the fence and Lump passed around some chocolate biscuits from his vast supply of tuck. Oh, it was good to be back together again. What a great bunch of mates we all were.

As people passed us they smiled and said hello. It's funny how you can suddenly change from being public enemy number one to being the best thing since sliced bread, I reflected.

Boy, my Dad had felt really stupid when he pieced together what had happened. He had actually taken

Mr Booth's word for it, when he and the Hulk claimed they were with the Chief Constable at the time Aunty Edna was knocked down. It wasn't true, of course. They *had* been there in the morning, but not the afternoon. Mind you, the Chief Constable was very embarrassed to find out that he had bought his son a stolen car. Not only was the Hulk in trouble, but Mr Booth would get a stiff sentence at the court too.

With all the publicity we had got over the Booth case, my mum reckoned I soon wouldn't be able to get through the door because of the size of my head. There's no pleasing parents!

Of course, it wasn't all good news. Nothing anybody could do would bring us back our club hut, but all the fuss had caused a lot of people in the church to think again about the use of the church hall. In fact, they had all pulled together and promised to buy us some new equipment, which was really nice of them considering the damage I had caused. I still blushed to think of the piano incident.

It wasn't just that they had changed, I had as well. You couldn't go through all the things that had happened to me and not be changed. Some of the things that had made Sparky the way he was had now started to become a part of my life. By talking to Doug and Sparky, I realized that God was actually interested in *me*, and how I lived. And that Jesus wasn't someone to get embarrassed about, or a name just used for swearing. Things were starting to make sense to me. Being a Christian wasn't about *trying* to be good, but something to do with trusting in Jesus. Already my bad temper was more under control. And I was starting to realize how bigheaded I had been. Poor old Doug was still in hospital, but he was nearly better. He had promised us a really great new club in the church hall. . .

I was woken from my dreaming by a warm, wet tongue. Staring me in the face was 'Wally'. He was my pride and joy! Dad had relented, and said I could have a dog. We had been to the Dogs' Home to choose one and of course I had to pick the oddest dog in the place. It was his look. You know, the look that says, 'I only want to be a friend, and if you take me away from here, I will worship you for ever.' He is a cross between an Old English Sheepdog and something else much smaller, and looks like a walking floor mop. He had to be called Wally!

'Oh, Wally,' I spluttered through the damp licking. 'Stop it, stop it!'

I turned to Little Mo, who was struggling at the other end of the lead. 'Sorry,' she said. 'I tried to take him to the park, but he heard your shout and dragged me this way.'

'It's all right,' I replied.

'We don't mind you at all,' I said to Wally. You really get daft with pets — as if he could understand! We all kept Wally entertained by throwing sticks out into the street, which he returned, his tail wagging, eyes bright, and giving the occasional deep 'Ruff'. Then Whizzer reminded us that we were in the middle of a game, and shouldn't we get on with the second half.

'OK,' I said cheerfully. 'I'll just tie Wally up to the lamppost.' 'Now you just stay there,' I said to him, 'and behave yourself.'

'Ruff,' he replied.

We carried on, with Little Mo joining my team. The ball bobbed about up and down the street, and we all tried to keep it away from Wally, who was attempting to play for both sides whenever it came near the lamppost. I had been teaching him to play nose football, and he showed a natural talent, but didn't have much goal sense. He tended to keep going in whichever direction the ball was going.

I was on the run again, hurtling down the pavement, Sparky facing me in defence. I closed in on him, with the ball at my feet. With the outside of my foot I flicked the ball against the wall, and slid past him on the other side. I controlled the ball again and looked up. Raj was standing by the goal, waiting.

'To my head, to my head,' he yelled.

Lump stood quaking by his side. Sam was running back to help.

I kicked the ball over to Raj, who leaped to head it just as Sam arrived to defend. Lump just stood there.

With an incredible crunch they all met. Raj was wedged between Sam and Lump like a sardine sandwich. The ball hit Raj's head, popped up in the air and gently sailed over the locked gate of Booth's garage.

There was a stunned silence. Sam, Raj, and Lump picked themselves up.

'Here we go again,' groaned Lump.

'What do we do now?' asked Chip.

'Well, *I'm* not going to try and climb over,' I said.

'Nor me,' added Whizzer.

'And I'm not going to let anybody use me as a stepladder,' grunted Lump.

There was a pause.

I really had to laugh, and what started as a chuckle, turned into uncontrollable laughter. The others joined in till we were all rolling about the street laughing. Eventually, when the laughing subsided, the inevitable question was asked.

'Well, what *are* we going to do to get the ball back?' Sam asked.

'You'll never guess where it's landed,' said Sparky as he looked through a gap between the fence post and the rest of the fence.

'Where?'

'It's lying by that heap of old tyres,' he said.

We all groaned. It brought back such memories.

'Ruff,' added Wally, who thought he had been forgotten. That gave me an idea. I untied him, and walked over to the gap.

'What are you up to?' asked Sparky.

'Wait and see,' I replied with a smirk.

'Now, Wally,' I said to the dog, 'go through the gap, fetch ball, fetch ball.'

'Ruff,' he responded.

I pushed him through the gap and, with wagging tail, he waddled over to the heap of tyres. 'Football, Wally, football,' I encouraged.

He nosed the ball, and began to push it away from the tyres. The only trouble was, he didn't have control or direction, so he just chased up and down the yard, wagging his tail. But eventually he came near enough for me to grab the ball through the fence and he followed it out, tail still wagging.

We patted and cheered him till he got thoroughly excited, which was a big mistake. He was leaping up and down for all he was worth. Whizzer kicked the ball away, and Wally was so excited he chased after it, and began his daft game of nose football all over again, this time down the street.

We all chased after him, yelling for him to stop. In the end we had him cornered and he stopped. However, as we closed in on him, he took it into his head that this was another game.

As I reached out for the ball he grabbed it in his teeth.

'No, Wally, no!' I yelled.

Too late! He might be stupid but he has really sharp teeth. The sound of air escaping from the football was unmistakable.

There was nothing for it. With a sigh, we all sat down. With a wagging tail and winning eyes Wally dropped the ball at my feet, punctured and useless.

We all looked at each other and laughed. Another disaster for Nick and Co!

Escape!

'There was a loud, fast chopping sound, as the helicopter roared over the spot where Tran had stood a moment before.

Machine-gun fire suddenly ripped the air. His pounding heart seemed to stop beating. Had they seen him?'

When the soldiers came, Tran and his family had to leave everything behind – their home, their town, their country.

Now Tran is alone in the jungle, and afraid.

This is the story of a long journey – a journey to saftey, to freedom and a new life.

**Mystery at Hawktowers
and other stories**

Adventure, mystery, danger, suspense are some of the ingredients in this exciting new collection of action-packed stories.

There's a Wild West adventure, a futuristic space story, a spine-chilling legend — and lots more!